THUMB PICKLES

AND OTHER
CAUTIONARY PRESERVES

DARCY-LEE TINDALE

JoJo
PUBLISHING

Thumb Pickles: and other Cautionary Preserves
Darcy-Lee Tindale

Published by Classic Author and Publishing Services Pty Ltd
An imprint of Jo Jo Publishing
First published 2014

'Yarra's Edge'
2203/80 Lorimer Street
Docklands VIC 3008
Australia

Email: jo-media@bigpond.net.au or visit www.classic-jojo.com

JoJo Publishing Imprint
Editor: Anne van Alkemade
Designer / typesetter: Working Type Studio (www.workingtype.com.au)

National Library of Australia Cataloguing-in-Publication entry
Author: Tindale, Darcy-Lee, author.
Title: Thumb pickles and other cautionary preserves / Darcy-Lee
                 Tindale ; designer, Luke Harris.
ISBN: 9780987609618 (paperback)
Target Audience: For secondary school age.
Subjects: Life skills--Juvenile fiction.
                 Advice in literature.
Other Authors/Contributors:
                 Harris, Luke, book designer.
Dewey Number: A823.4

These are the stories you won't believe,
and the stories your parents don't want you to believe.

Acknowledgements

To Mum and Dad; thanks for giving me the thumbs up!

To Ethan; take good care of your digits (and use them to clean your room!).

Thank you to my editor, Anne van Alkemade. You are the green thumb of editing.

The following stories were first published in The NSW Department of Education THE SCHOOL MAGAZINE; one-time serial rights.

1. Eating carrots helps you see in the dark
   The truth behind myth #1 (*Orbit* Oct Issue, 2013)
2. If you don't wash your dirty ears, you'll end up growing potatoes
   The truth behind myth #3 (*Touchdown* Nov Issue, 2012)

Pickled Thumbs:
and other cautionary preserves

'Lies can be the perfect cure to help others stay out of trouble'

Author's note:

I am about to tell you four stories. Before I begin, I must be honest and tell you that three of these stories are lies and only one of the four stories is true. You may be wondering, *what is the point of telling a story if it's not true?* And the answer to that is, it is not the story, but the reason why the story is told that is important.

Sometimes lies are told for good reasons. There are lessons in them. They can be the perfect cure to help others stay out of trouble and are told to teach a moral of sorts, a lesson to the listener. I understand this contradicts what you have been taught — never tell a fib, a falsehood, or diddle and most certainly don't ever tell a whopper, fat bogie, or mammoth porkpie, but these lies or myths are told for many a good reason. Some lies are entertaining, some are funny and some are strange or spooky or sad — but they all have a lesson.

Perhaps I should say no more and tell the four tales.

I'll let you decide which story is the lie and which is the truth. Or perhaps you will think that all of them are just horrid fabrications, horrendous hoaxes, duck-decoys, silly lies told only to entertain and to teach. No matter, as long as they fill their purpose. And the best thing of all, you get to pick the lesson!

Perhaps I should give you a little forewarning before you begin. Remember, even villains can fall in love.

Here Endeth the Prologue of This Book

Here Beginneth The Carrot Tale

The truth behind myth #1

"Zee carrots vill change zee vay you see! True! Noh?
If you do not eat zee carrots, you vill not see in zee dark. Ja?"
Fräulein Von Fohn – 1912

Translation: *"Eating carrots will help you see in the dark"*

Fräulein Von Fohn lived in the heart of a busy town called Radmustdish, in the middle of the country called Jarmoney. She lived with her husband, Klaus Von Fohn, a large and sometimes very smelly man. Klaus was large and smelly because of what he loved to eat. He would eat pork and chicken and cabbage and potatoes. He would eat things with very strange names like *sahnemeerrettich* and *pumpernickel* and *schupfnudel*. It's true! I'm not making these words up! He would eat anything, as long as it was smeared in mustard and horseradish.

Klaus loved mustard. He would put mustard on his toast in the morning and smear it on his eggs.

Sometimes he would spread it straight off the butter knife onto his tongue. What Klaus liked more than mustard was horseradish.

HOW TO MAKE HORSERADISH
From the horseradish plant, toss the plant
but keep the plant roots.
Grate the plant roots and mix in vinegar.
Pour mixture over EVERYTHING!
Eat!

Klaus would cover his meat and all his vegetables in horseradish. The hotter the horseradish and mustard, the more Klaus would eat.

Klaus loved mustard and horseradish so much that he saved all his coins and kept them in a jar. Once a month he would go into town with his jar of money and buy every bottle and pot of mustard and horseradish in the town's store. Klaus was the only person in Radmustdish who had ever tasted mustard and horseradish. That was because he never shared them with anyone else. He would also always forget to buy his wife a lollypop from the store before returning home.

What Fräulein Von Fohn hated (aside from missing out on her lollypops) was the smell of her husband when he was eating mustard and horseradish.

"You smell!" Fräulein would cry.

"*Danke*," Klaus would reply.

But what Klaus hated was carrots. No matter how much horseradish or mustard he added, no matter how spicy or hot the horseradish or mustard, Klaus could still taste carrot.

"Eat your carrots," Fräulein would cry.

"*Nein!*" Klaus would reply.

As the years passed, Klaus became bigger and smellier, until none of Fräulein's friends wanted to visit any more. Poor Fräulein became lonely. The only company she had were the toads in her front garden. So she befriended them.

Klaus was horrified. "You vill not play vit zee frogs, Fräulein Von Fohn. Zay vill give you vorts!" he cried.

"Ven you stop eating mustard and horseradish, I vill stop playing vit zee toads," replied Fräulein.

But as the years passed, Klaus kept eating mustard and horseradish, and Fräulein kept playing with the toads. In fact, Klaus ate more mustard and radish — spicier mustard and hotter horseradish. Fräulein continued to play with her toads, but she did not seem to grow any warts.

One cold wintery day, the house was warm, and the windows fogged. Poor old Fräulein, now grey-haired, could not see out the windows.

Alone with just her toads, she cried, "Klaus! Zee

fog on zee inside of the vindows must be caused by your bad breath!"

Klaus replied, "Nonsense! But if you keep playing wit zee toads you vill be covered in vorts!"

"Nonsense!" replied Fräulein.

That night, at the dinner table, as Fräulein and Klaus sat down to eat, Fräulein placed her napkin on her lap and Klaus opened a new jar of mustard and a new jar of horseradish. But the jars of mustard and horseradish were so hot, the spice so zesty, the piquancy so strong, that the fumes wafted up into Klaus's eyes before he even took a bite. So intense was the odour, so extraordinarily scorching was the heat, that Klaus's eyes suddenly began to water badly. Suddenly he could not see a thing.

Klaus screwed up his eyes and yelped, "I am blind!"

Seeing her one opportunity, Fräulein Von Fohn quickly turned off all the lights, plunging the house into darkness.

"Fräulein! Fräulein! Did you hear me? I'm blind! Vat shall I do? I cannot see!" cried Klaus.

"Eat zee carrots," cried Fräulein. "Eat zee *carrots!*"

His eyes streaming with tears, Klaus thought he had been blinded by the heat and spice from the mustard and horseradish. So he felt he had no choice: he began to shovel carrot after carrot into his mouth. Fräulein Von Fohn, on the other hand, snatched up all the left-over jars of horseradish and seeded mustard that she could find in the house and smeared their contents all over her face, arms, legs and neck, all the while yelling to her husband, "More carrots! Eat more of zee carrots!"

At last the scent of mustard and horseradish faded from the air and Klaus's eyes stopped watering. Fräulein turned the lights back on. Miraculously, Klaus could see again.

As Klaus wiped away his tears, he saw his wife covered in horseradish and mustard, so he instantly ate her!

No, he didn't. Just joking. Here's what really happened.

Klaus turned and looked at his wife. Seeing her covered in hideous lumps and bumps, he gasped, "Fräulein! Vot is vrong vit your skin?"

"Ah! You see, all those carrots have made your eyes much better. Even better zan before. So good, in fact, zat at last you can really see. Ja, finally you can see me clearly!"

"But vot is vrong vit your skin?"

"It must be vorts from playing vit zee toads all these years!" Fräulein replied.

"Then you must stop playing vit zee toads," cried Klaus.

"Okay, okay! I vill stop playing vit zee frogs and

toads, if you stop eating zee mustard and horserad-ish," answered Fräulein.

Klaus agreed.

"See, I told you," said Fräulein, "zee carrots vill change zee vay you see! True! *Nein?* If you do not eat zee carrots, you vill not see in zee dark. Ja? Now you see!"

Later that night, Klaus ate his supper of *sahn-emeerrettich, schupfnudel* and *pumpernickel* with salt and pepper, and they tasted just as delicious without smothering his food in mustard and horseradish.

"Zis food is vonderful," said Klaus.

Fräulein blushed, *"Danke."*

Then Fräulein took a shower to wash off all the horseradish and mustard before Klaus had a chance to figure out her trickery.

Over the rest of their years together, Klaus started to smell better. Once a month he visited the town's store to buy his wife a lollypop. And because their windows no longer fogged up, people could see that they were home and visitors stopped by.

Fräulein was happy that she had friends to visit once more and that Klaus no longer smelt. She never told her husband that carrots don't make you see in the dark, but lights do, and because of her little lie, both Klaus and Fräulein lived happily ever after.

Here endeth the Fräulein tale

Here Beginneth the Wind Tale

The truth behind myth #2

*"Lemme tell you; If you pull'a da face anda da wind change,
you're gonna be stuck like that foreve'a!"*
– Bella Fragranza — 1725

Translation: *"If you pull a face and the wind changes,
you'll be stuck like that forever."*

Bella Fragranza lived in a country near southern
Europe called Itisalie, in a tiny village on the south
side called Gluh. Bella was a little woman who loved
to cook big meals. All day in her kitchen she would be
boiling, broiling, steaming, mashing, rolling, sifting,
mixing, sniffing, tasting and at the end of the day —
the part she loved the most — she would be serving.

Bella loved to fill her dinner table with glorious
food. Her meals were like art. Each dish should have
been on display in the Uffizi Gallery. On the crisp
white linen, bright hand-painted pottery bowls were
piled high of *agnolotti*. Each half-circular pasta shape

was stuffed with meat and in perfect form as the next. Some of her *agnolotti* looked like fairy pillows, so soft and enticing, you could almost curl up and rest your head on them. Her chopped salad was so colourful, it equalled the beauty of the rolling hills outside her windows. The fragrance from the table would waft and fill the room, spill from her windows and make the villagers' mouths water. "What is for your husband's supper tonight, Bella?" came calls from envious men as they returned from their day's labour.

"Tonight, *crostini*, made with red pepper and capers for starter, then deep-fried courgette flowers to tickle my husband's tongue."

"Ah! He must be more handsome than the god *Anteros* to be made such a feast," came the reply.

Bella was not finished yet, "then *tortellini* filled with wild mushrooms and spinach risotto cake."

"So much for one husband!" cried another voice from the path below.

"He must be more spoiled than the god *Comus!*"

"Then a sweet *panforte* with a tart espresso coffee."

"All this for one man?" Their voices chimed.

"And last," sang Bella to the voices outside her window, "before bed, to cool the body's temperature, *blood orange granita.*"

"Ah!" sighed the men.

Yes, all of this, just for her husband.

The envious men walked on.

Bella loved to serve, she was born to serve.

Every night she served delightful, delicious, delectable meals to her small, stumpy, stupido husband.

Si!

Each night her husband would gorge her meals, fill his belly, slurp, burp and lick his lips, while Bella Fragranza watched with anticipation, waiting with baited breath for a response to her meal.

And at the end of every feast she would ask in her small voice, "Signor, was tonight's meal delizioso?"

And for twenty years, night after night, at the end of every meal, this ungrateful, tomato head, stupido man, would wipe his mouth, purse his lips, sway his head, screw up his face and say ...

"Lemme think, eh! Hmm ... too much salt!"

Or twist his face, scratch his chin, roll his eyes and say, "I know watsa matter, not enough flavour tonight!"

Or he would give a distorted smirk, shrug his shoulders, before slurping the last of the sauce from the bottom of his bowl, then pucker his lips and say, "Dunno, maybe a little over done for my liking. It oughta be cooked a liddle less."

Or he'd crinkle his forehead, wriggle his fingers, then snort like an ox and grunt, "I ain't one to complain, but, eh, perhaps a touch more herbs!"

And back in her kitchen, Bella Fragranza would roll and kneed, and dust, and sweat, and taste and broil and boil, and boil, and boil.

Then one night, Bell Fragranza's small hand shook as she touched her forehead, then touched her tiny belly button, then her shoulder, then her other shoulder with the little brown mole, and then she pressed her palms together and closed her eyes and smiled. Her little lips moved quickly, but made no sound. Then she opened her eyes and spent the next four hours sifting with the silkiest fluffy white flour, whisking with the freshest eggs, stolen and still warm from under the chooks. Bella Fragranza's gentle loving hands, folded, and kneaded, and dusted and strung perfect, *perfecto* pasta.

In a pot of boiling water with a pinch of salt and a dash of olive oil she boiled the pasta. To test its perfection, she took a spaghetti strand from the pot and tossed it up at the roof and it stuck to the kitchen ceiling instantly in the shape of a heart.

Bella Fragranza knew her pasta was *al dente*!

Her pot bubbled away with tomato, basil and many other small secrets that had been handed from her great, great grandmother, all the way down to her trusted kitchen.

At last, it was done. Bella stepped lightly towards the dining table and on her finest platter she served the meal to her husband and waited, and waited, and waited.

Her husband slurped, he sucked and burped, this meal was truly *delizimo.*

Absolute *perfecto.*

It was a *masterpiece!*

With wide eyes Bella Fragranza asked, "Well? Signor?"

And her husband, Signor Stupido, began

        to

           screw

              up

                his

                    face!

"Nooooh!" cried Bella Fragranza, "Lemme tell you; if you pull'a face anda da wind changes, you're gonna be stuck like that foreve'a!"

And for a fleeting moment, with a tender smile on his face and love in his heart, Signor Stupido said to his wife, "Oh, Signora Bella, eh, you make me laugh!" and then his face twisted and distorted as he blurted, "and then I will choke on my meal!"

And that last remark was enough for Bella Fragranza. Her face went as red as a tomato.

That night Bella Fragranza waited until Signor Stupido went to bed, then she tip toed into the kitchen. And with flour and not eggs, and water instead, she did not make pasta, but glue! And while Signor Stupido's face distorted and twisted as he snored, she painted his face with this homemade glue.

The next morning, Signora Bella Fragranza hummed loudly and smiled as she fried bacon and eggs. She poured in three scoops of salt. She added grated parsnip, she crumpled dried fish flakes, she dropped in three cloves of garlic and two chillies, whilst adding the scrapings from the bottom of a dirty boot. And as she whistled, she added one chook feather, and a jar of green tomato and gherkin pickles!

"Signor, your breakfast is ready!"

"*Grazie*," came the reply.

Signor Stupido sat and shovelled a great hunk of food into his mouth, chewed, then instantly twisted up his face. "Eh! This is *disgustoso!*"

Bella Fragranza quickly threw open the kitchen window shutters letting in a great gush of air. "Careful Signor, if you pull'a the face anda da wind changes, you're gonna be stuck like'a that foreve'a — now eat!"

Signor shovelled in another mouthful, only to scrunch up his face even tighter and cry, "It tastes orrible!"

Just then a huge gust of wind whistled as it blew into the kitchen, parting the lace curtains framing the window like twin ghosts and the glue at last dried on Signor Stupido's hideous face.

"Ah, too late!" cried Bella Fragranza. "Your face is gonna be stuck like that foreve'a!"

"Noh. It can't be *corretto*?"

"*Preciso!*"

And in the reflection of his gooey yellow egg, Signor Stupido saw how his face would look forever — and it was NOT sunny side up!

"No matter," shrugged Bella Fragranza looking up at the ceiling, "I still love you."

"Really?" asked Signor Stupido.

Bella Fragranza swallowed, her small hand shook as she touched her forehead, then her tiny belly button, then her shoulder, then her other shoulder with the little brown mole, and then she pressed her palms together and smiled, "Tis true!"

Here endeth the bella her tale

Here Beginneth the Dirty Ears Tale

The truth behind myth #3

"If ye don' be washin' behind ye ears yer be grow'n potatoes in 'em."
Lorcan O'Reilly — 1882

Translation: *"If you don't wash behind your ears potatoes will grow in them"*

Lorcan O'Reilly was an Oirishman, who lived in Oiriland, a small country that sat near the edge of the Atlantic Ocean. It was always cold and wet in Oiriland, but at least the grass was always green.

In the heart of Oiriland was a small village called Parsnip Place, where Lorcan O'Reilly lived with his wife, Emma O'Reilly, and his son, Fergus O'Reilly.

Lorcan O'Reilly owned a farm. And on that farm,

he grew potatoes. And to feed his family he sold these potatoes. And to save money he made his son dig the potatoes from the ground. His son, Fergus, *hated* digging for potatoes.

Digging up potatoes is extremely dirty work. Because potatoes grow in — of all things — dirt! So every day after Fergus O'Reilly dug potatoes from the ground, he was, well, dirty! And every night before going to bed Fergus had a bath to wash away this dirt. Fergus would bathe in a small copper tub that hardly fitted his legs, so he had to bend his knees and point them up towards the sky. He would wash between his toes, around his legs and over his body. He would remember to wash behind his knees and under his arms. He would wash his neck and his face. However, by the time he got to his ears the water was cold. Freezing cold. The water would be so icy cold that Fergus would skip washing behind his ears and pull the plug, letting the muddy water swill down the drain.

After many months of not washing behind his ears, Fergus had very dirty, very smelly, mouldy, fungus-filled ears.

His father could take no more of it and started calling him Fungus instead of Fergus — purely by mistake of course.

Both Lorcan and Emma O'Reilly no longer hugged

their child, because of the putrid smell. It made them heave and gag. Poor Fergus had almost forgotten what a hug felt like and was very thankful for his dog, the only thing left that would come near him.

Nevertheless, Fergus still refused to wash behind his ears. Then one day his father said, "If ye don' be washin' behind ye ears, Fungus, yer be grown' potatoes."

Fergus laughed at this nonsense and went to bed with dirty ears.

The next morning Fergus woke up to find a small potato on his pillow.

"Ma! Da! Oi found me a wee potato on me piller," cried Fergus.

"Musta fallen out from behind yer ear durin' de noight," replied Lorcan O'Reilly.

Fergus was not completely convinced that this could be true. However, the next morning when he woke up he found another, slightly bigger, potato on his pillow.

"Ma! Da! Oi found me another potato," cried Fergus.

"Oi keep tellin' ye, son, dey be fallin' out from behind yer ears," said Lorcan O'Reilly.

Fergus, still not yet convinced, refused to wash behind his ears.

Every morning when Fergus woke, there was

another potato and every morning they seemed to be bigger and bigger and bigger.

"Oi'd be washin' behind yer ears, son, before de potatoes get so big dey squashes yer head!"

Fergus was starting to worry and by now the smell wafting from behind his ears was putrid.

That night, while Fergus slept in his bed, Lorcan O'Reilly — just like he had done every other night since Fergus found the first potato — crept out into the field to dig up another potato. Only this time he dug up the largest potato he could find. Lorcan O'Reilly carried the potato back over his shoulder and placed it gently on his son's pillow. You see, Mr O'Reilly was trying to teach his son a lesson.

The next morning Fergus woke with a start — and an enormous potato!

"Father! Father! De potatoes be growing bigger than me head! Father! Father! Come quick."

Lorcan O'Reilly raced into his son's room, but as he entered, he was so overcome by the revolting stench of dirty ears. It turned his stomach, made is throat twitch and nostrils burn. Lorcan O'Reilly could hardly breathe and became dizzy and gagged from the repulsive smell.

At that moment, his wife, Emma O'Reilly, entered the room and asked, "What do yer think de Moon be made of?"

And because he could think of no other word to describe the smell, Lorcan O'Reilly's last dying words were, 'Cheese!'

(Okay, he didn't really die. I just made that up for dramatic effect. He fainted from the revolting smell of rotten cheese.)

Three days later, when Lorcan O'Reilly finally came to, he discovered that his wife had scraped all the dirt, mould and fungus from behind her son's ears. Fergus smelt clean, fresh and at last was now huggable again. Emma O'Reilly (after giving her son lots and lots of hugs to make up for the ones he missed while he stunk) said her son would never have to dig another potato again as long as he kept his ears clean. Fergus agreed and he and his mother shook hands on it, and then hugged on it.

Inspired by the Moon being made of cheese, Emma O'Reilly rolled up the gunk she had collected from behind Fergus' ear into the shape of the full moon and in this way she created blue vein cheese. And the O'Reillys became rich, selling blue vein cheese to the world, with a side of fig preserve and mango pickle.

Here endeth the lorcan his tale

Here Beginneth The Thumb Thief Tale

The truth behind myth #4

"If you keep sucking your thumb, the great Thumb Thief will come and chop it clean off."
Harriet, the daughter of the Mayor of Tenderville

Translation: *"If you take things for granted and don't look after them, you might end up losing them — thumbs and friends included."*

Not many people know that all small country towns have something they are proud of. For instance, in the tiny town of Nundle the town folk are proud of their wool mill, gold flecks found in the nearby creek and the birth of a two headed goat — that's right — a goat was born with two heads and the town just loved it, or should I say, loved *them*.

But this story is not set in Nundle, it is set in the small town of Tenderville, not even close to Nundle, in fact, the two towns probably have never even heard of each other.

In the small town of Tenderville they also had things they were proud of; like their cherry blossom trees that lined the main street of town and flowered in spring; and their grapes and orange orchards that grew along the hillside, stretching as far as the eye could see. Tenderville thrived on the orange orchards and grapevines. It was how the town made its living. In fact, the town was so proud, at the end of every harvesting season Tenderville would celebrate their success of growing ripe and delicious grapes and oranges at an annual Grape and Orange festival.

The town would hang huge banners that draped over the road. They would have a street parade with band music and marching girls. And floats, where the people who stood on them were dressed up in costumes and waved to the crowd below. Some floats even tossed candy out into the crowd.

After the street parade, there was the official opening by the town's Mayor in the fairground and the town's people would beam with pride.

"Keeps the town clock turning," Mr Hollingsworth would say.

"Tenderville makes the best grape and orange juice

this side of the country," said all the fathers that worked in the orchards.

"Keeps our husbands busy," said the wives of the husbands.

"Keeps our thirst at bay," said the children of the wives and husbands.

"Has made the town what it is today," said the old Mayor.

Everyone in Tenderville was happy; very, very happy.

For twenty-six years Tenderville held its annual festival, a great fete of sorts, in the town's fairground and everyone would spend the whole weekend celebrating with music, pony rides and paddle boats in the nearby dam. There would be face painting, food (mostly grapes and oranges) and more importantly, the town celebrated its ability to work together and its friendships.

The town of Tenderville had declared their own public holiday, calling it Grape and Orange Day. This wasn't a clever name by any means, but it was their day and the town was proud to have it. The orchard owners would give all their workers the Monday morning off after the fair, so they could rest before the new season cycle started again.

On this particular day, the twenty-sixth to be exact, the newest Mayor of Tenderville and his lovely young wife proudly opened the festival. Before climbing up onto the stage with the squeaky microphone, the Mayor's wife told him he was the most amazing man a woman could ever wish to marry and the new town Mayor laughed and tapped her nose and joked, "Ops, I think your nose just grew a little longer, dear."

Now, you may be wondering, what is so interesting about all of this? Everyone is happy, the town *is* called Tenderville after all and you would be absolutely right. But sometimes while we look up into the blue sky and enjoy the warmth of the sun and the possibilities ahead as far as our eyes can see and dream, near our feet are tiny spiders spinning webs to catch small grass insects to eat, centipedes are crawling under rocks, lizards are flicking their tongues waiting for a fly to pass by and leeches are hiding under sticks, just waiting to slither into our socks and latch onto our ankles and suck our blood, and then there are slugs that leave trails.

While the whole of Tenderville was looking up at the new town Mayor trying to speak into the high pitch squeaky microphone, perhaps they should have been looking at the small baby that crawled about between their feet, amongst the centipedes, spiders and leeches. But no one did.

Up on the stage, the Mayor thanked everyone and showed his appreciation of being elected the new town Mayor. His speech waffled on a little bit about his election promises, which was long and boring and made all the children fidget, and then it made all the mothers sigh and slap the knees of the fidgeting children when they thought other people were not looking at them, and then it made the fathers give the children 'the-look' but still the new Mayor — having no children of his own yet — babbled on and on. But if you know and understand anything about politics, this is what one would expect. At last the Mayor thanked Mr Hollingsworth, the town's handyman, for his hard work in building the new picnic benches to help celebrate 'this momentous' occasion, and the audience applauded Mr Hollingsworth.

Pew! The speeches were over and the Mayor smiled at the glow of pride from his newly-married wife, and declared the twenty-sixth festival officially open.

From a chain that hung from his waist coat, that also held his wallet (which had just enough money to buy some crusty bread, cheese and a bottle of red wine and pay the week's rent), and a watch that was once his great-great-grandfathers, there was a small pair of second hand brass scissors — a gift from his wife — to cut the ribbon and announce the official start of the celebrations.

The Mayor held the brass scissors up towards the sky, and as he did he saw the small baby crawling in the grass below. As he snipped the ribbon he whispered the child's name, '*Archor*' and both these words and the ribbon lifted up into the wind and drifted above the town of Tenderville and across the orchards of the town.

Later that afternoon, baby Archor sat in the sandpit and licked sand from his fingers. He wiggled his pinkie finger and poked it into the sand, he licked and poked his ring finger into the sand, and he slobbered over his middle finger, drooled and sucked on his pointer finger as it wiggled inside his toothless mouth, but Archor did *not* suck his thumb — because he didn't have one. Archor didn't have either of his thumbs. He was born thumbless.

Now you would think if you were missing a thumb and the place where you should be growing a thumb, wasn't growing a thumb, that it would look hideous or grotesque or ugly. You might think the empty spot where the thumb should be would look repulsive and make a person almost look monstrous. But that was *not* the case. Archor was *perfectly* thumbless. The place where his thumbs should have been was smooth and flowing, almost like a perfect hand without the intrusion of a protruding thumb. No place on his hand showed a hint of where a thumb should grow; his hand was perfectly proportioned with fingers. Archor's perfectly thumbless handmade thumb people feel uncomfortable.

As baby Archor lolled about in the sandpit like all babies like to do, the mothers one by one removed their children and in no time at all Archor was the only child left in the sandpit. Not only was Archor perfectly thumbless, he was perfectly friendless.

And Archor's mum, Mrs Chatelaine, who was now becoming used to people's reactions, assured them that his condition wasn't infectious. (Being thumbless is not a disease). He was, nevertheless, left isolated because of other people's reactions when they saw her thumbless baby.

"Never mind, Archor," said Mrs Chatelaine. "I want you to know, you can't count your friends on your hands, but only in your heart. So you don't need all those extra digits anyway."

As baby Archor snuggled into the arms of his mother and the two left the fairground alone, he had no idea of the stares of the people, the whispers and the murmurs, the mocking and the sneers at the monstrous baby with the missing thumbs — but rest assured, all of that would come later in his life.

Maybe Mrs Chatelaine had an inkling of what might happen and as she slipped out of the fairground onto the main street and walked along the road lined with cherry blossoms she whispered into her son's ear, "Don't ever let other people's words become your compass, Archor." And as the evening wind blew, pink blossom petals sprinkled the path towards home.

That night Archor lay in his crib and like all clever babies, he clapped hands for his mother. Only when it came time to fall asleep, because Archor had no thumbs to suck, he would spend the rest of the night crying until poor Mrs Chatelaine lent him her thumb to suck.

On this dreary night, as the rain pattered on the window outside, Mrs Chatelaine was in desperate need of sleep. She wanted to curl up in her own bed, and tuck her thumbs under her pillow and sleep, and sleep and sleep, but Archor was used to his substitute thumbs and every time Mrs Chatelaine tried to slowly withdraw her thumb from Archor's mouth — WHAH!

Archor's cries would fill the room and his mother's head and she wished she had a magic wand that would put her son to sleep. And in that small wish she had found her answer.

On the shelf above Archor's bed was indeed a magic wand. Mrs Chatelaine smiled, she had found a solution. She gave Archor the magic wand that originally belonged to his father. Instead of sucking his mothers thumb, Archor's small baby fingers cupped the wand perfectly and he made small whimpering noises of satisfaction as he sucked the tip of the wand and fell asleep — like magic.

"See, Archor, there is magic in having no thumbs," said Mrs Chatelaine, then she kissed Archor's forehead and whispered, "In the darkness we are all the same, Archor." Then she turned out the light and went to bed and enjoyed a lovely, long night of sleep.

Little did Mrs Chatelaine know that by giving her son this wand it would be the beginning of her son's fascination with all things magic.

Archor at eight and a half

Archor grew from a baby into a toddler and then a small child. By the age of eight and a half, Archor learnt his numbers, alphabet, hand writing, reading, how to ride a bike, fly a kite, make paper aeroplanes, paint, bake cookies and lots more, without needing thumbs.

Archor had also made friends. Two. Morden was Archor's best friend (the second friend we will meet later on in the story). Morden was also an only child, just like Archor, only Morden thought Archor's mother was kind and caring, and thought his own mother was strange and very confusing. His mother would tell him every morning that all she wanted for him was to grow up and be happy, and then she would spend the rest of the day nagging and yelling at him. His mother was also sarcastic and Morden was too young to understand sarcasm or irony. He didn't realise that when his mother spoke to him, she actually meant the complete opposite of what she said. On this particular morning, Morden's mother left a very *sarcastic* letter on Morden's bedroom door.

Morden, I keep telling you, please, stop
cleaning up your room!

(a note written by Morden's mother and pinned to Morden's bedroom door with an old dart that the family dog had once chewed, but is still in perfect working order, should any of his friends wish to come over for a game of darts!)

Morden! Now the zombies think that you're
creating a brand new smelling perfume,
and I'd hate to see you disappoint them, and
come to your doom,
so Morden, I beg you, please, oh please, just
don't clean up your room!

Please leave the dust and the dirt, that
resembles *Mt Everest* that looms,
because I truly enjoy crawling around in there,
with not an inch of any legroom,
and I'm always surprised and delighted, to find
a thousand used teaspoons,

and filthy plates, with something
un-recognisable you ate,
that has regrown and begun to bloom!

Morden, I have to tell you, please, don't ever
clean up your room!
I truly enjoy the mummified apples, like the
ones found in *El Faiyum*,
and the dog is pleased that someone has finally
had him exhumed,
he was panting and puffing under all your
clothes, thinking he'd forever be entombed.

Oh, Morden please, let's make it clear, don't
ever clean up your room!
Never mind the floor, for I am sure, it's never
seen a brush or a broom,
oh, is that carpet down there? Oh well, no need
to clog up the old vacuum?
And those dirty plates, hardly understates, the
rooms powerful feeling of gloom,
oh, Morden please, let's make it clear, don't
ever clean up your room!

Oh, sorry dear, am I yelling? Oh, well, I'll try to
turn down my volume.

Now back to your mess, to your dirty life, your
living style may resume,
because who am I to rant and rave, and be a par-
ent that fumes?
So hugs and kisses, sorry to disturb, let's call it a
truce, and we'll both continue to presume,
that I'm perfectly happy, don't mind me, I totally
agree, no, don't ever clean up your room!

Morden read the letter and not wanting his mother to yell at him, he did exactly what the letter asked
him to do — and Morden did *not* clean up his room.
Instead he jumped on his push bike and went for a
ride down town.

*   *   *

Archor was the complete opposite to his friend Morden. Archor thought it was strange when his mother
did perfectly normal things and he thought it was
normal when his mother did very strange things. On
this particular morning, Archor thought his mother's behaviour at breakfast was strange — all because
she was acting as normal as possible.

For example, earlier that morning when Archor's
mother went upstairs to open her son's bedroom
door to wake him, the door knob disappeared.

That's right. It vanished right before her eyes — gone!

But Archor's mother did not squeal with fright or laugh with delight. Instead, she simply called, "Your breakfast is ready, and don't dilly dally or it will go cold."

"Humph," answered Archor.

Of course the door knob didn't actually disappear. Archor had rigged the brass door knob up to a pulley system. A very clever pulley system. A double tackle to be precise. It had two wheels and one heavy weight. When Mrs Chatelaine climbed the last step her foot hooked a near invisible fine fishing line that was attached to the pulley and heavy weight. The closer to the door she moved the more the rope hoisted the door knob up towards the roof and began to inch out of its socket, at the same time the weight attached to the rope went down towards the floor. You see, just as Mrs Chatelaine reached out her hand to grab the door knob, the tension on the wire was so tight that the knob popped out and disappeared. A really neat trick that deserved a much better reaction than Archor received.

"See you downstairs at the table," called Mrs Chatelaine, and Archor knew he needed to perform an even better trick to get a reaction from his mother.

Downstairs at the breakfast table, Mrs

Chatelaine was busy sewing a dark pink satin trim to the bottom of a very pretty lime green cotton dress. The lounge room (which should have been a place where Archor and his mother sat and read and relaxed, was instead a room filled with cotton reels, an old foot peddle sewing machine and yards and yards of material). Late into the night, Mrs Chatelaine would sew, snip, hem and cut out delicate dress patterns by a small kerosene lamp. Often Archor would ask, "Mum, why do you nearly go blind and let your finger tips prick and bleed just to make pretty dresses for everyone in town except yourself?"

And Archor's mother would always reply, "Oh, I don't see pretty dresses, Archor, I see something so fragile and delicate as a thread of cotton being able to hold a whole garment together. One tiny piece of cotton thread can strengthen and hold another person's dreams. I think that's where the magic is. In these little coloured bobbins and cotton reels."

And Archor thought his mother was strange. Fancy thinking there was any magic in a cotton reel. Archor loved magic, but real magic. Magic that only a clever and quick eye or another magician would know. That was better magic than cotton that held a dress together.

Mrs Chatelaine hung the dress over the back of

her chair and sat down at the table to have breakfast with her son. Under the table, Archor rubbed the sleeve of his woollen jumper as fast as he could against his pants to create a static charge. Then with his other hand he sprinkled pepper over his poached eggs, "Abracadabra!" Archor waved his hand over his eggs and suddenly all the black pepper on top of his eggs disappeared, "Ta-dah!"

"Well done, dear," replied his mother.

Archor's shoulders sagged, "You weren't even watching."

"Oh, Archor, all magic can be explained. You just need to know how. And you have obviously worked that one out."

Little did Archor know, this was a trick his mother had watched performed many times, many, many years ago when she shared breakfast with Archor's father.

As Archor dusted the black pepper off his sleeve, his mother picked up her breakfast knife, and as fast as she could she rubbed it against her own woollen sleeve, creating a mass of static electricity and then as she went to slice her poached egg in half all the pepper disappeared off her egg. "Ta-tah," said Mrs Chatelaine. The static charge had drawn all the pepper to the knife, but to someone who had never seen this trick done before, just like magic, her poached egg was pepper-less. But Archor was already wounded, and he hardly raised a smile.

"I think I taught you that one, Archor. But chin up, you are much cleverer at it than I am."

"Can I leave a little earlier for the fair today? Morden and Lilac want to get a good picnic spot."

"Sure. I still need to put on the finishing touches to this dress for the Mayor's wife. I'll catch up with you later, if you like."

Archor was half way out of his chair, when his mother touched his elbow and motioned for him to sit back down, "Before you race off, let me tell you a short story ..."

A short story by Mrs Chatelaine

There once was a lady who had banished herself from a village long before reaching eighty years of age. Each day of her life, for many years, she'd grown more and more spiteful towards the world. Her son had long ago become a great inventor and left the village to help others. The more distance there was between them, the more malicious, nasty and cruel she became, and the nastier the world grew towards her. Her face began to reflect her thoughts, reflected her feelings of bitterness and the world reflected it right back at her.

One day, a child walked all the way to the top of the mountain where the old lady lived all alone. The child knocked on her door and when the old lady answered the door the child asked, "What would it take for you to be kind, caring and gentle? For your face to soften and for you to be happy?"

The old lady replied, "A hug."

The child hugged the old lady and the pain and sadness, the bitterness and sorrow inside the old lady's heart began to melt away and for the first time in many, many years, a tiny drop of water fell from the duct in the corner of her eye.

Archor's mother's short stories always seemed to leave him feeling long in the face.

"Thanks, Mum." Archor kissed his mother on the cheek, then he gave her a big hug. He picked up the last triangular piece of toast from his plate and soaked up the gooey egg yolk from his plate, then disappeared out the front door. He munched on the toast as he made his way up the footpath and when he finished swallowing down the last bit of crust he noticed a napkin poking out of his sleeve. His mother had magically tucked the napkin there (without him even knowing) to wipe the yolk from around his mouth. At last, Archor smiled.

Tenderville's 34th Annual Orange and Grape Festival

Morden, Lilac (Archor's second friend, who we will now meet) and Archor did find a perfect spot to sit at the fair. Tucked away deep in the foliage of a willow tree, the three sat on a check pattern blanket in the cool shade and watched the events taking place across the fairground. They liked this spot the best because they thought the trees looming branches would conceal them, and then nobody would take any notice of them. Across the fairground there were many children sitting in little groups eating, chatting, giggling and playing, but Morden, Lilac and Archor instead hid, because these three seemed to stand out. They were not like the other children and drew attention to themselves, because one was smart, one was beautiful, and one was different.

All the while that Benjamin, Cornelius and Ivy nibbled on chicken drumsticks, William guzzled soft drink, Elton licked toffee and Jacinta let pink floss melt on her tongue, Katie poked twigs down ant holes, and Joan pulled a button off her dress and went searching for it in the tall grass, nobody seemed to pay any attention to Morden, Lilac and Archor, but everyone seemed to notice the three little children sitting in the shadows of the old willow tree. Even the town Mayor couldn't bring himself to ignore the distraction of these three children.

By his side stood his wife. She was wearing her beautiful new maternity dress that Archor's mother had put the last touches on that very morning. The Mayor's wife was expecting her third child. This baby would be born in the next month, and this delighted her daughter who was six years of age, but not the youngest child, a boy aged four.

"Babies stink," the four year old said to his father.

"Yes, indeed they do," the Mayor agreed.

"Babies vomit," the four year old said.

"Yes, they do that too," the Mayor replied.

"Babies make too much noise," the four year old said.

"Yes, they do, but we still love them," the Mayor replied.

The Mayor's daughter, Harriet, stuck her tongue

out at her brother for being so negative about the new baby that would soon enter their home. The Mayor tried to grab his daughter's tongue (but a slimy wet tongue is awfully hard to grab hold of), then the Mayor said, "Keep your tongue in your mouth, Harriet. I knew a child once that stuck out her tongue and wriggled it, and a black crow thought it was a worm coming out of a hole. The crow swooped down and swallowed the child's tongue in one gulp!"

Harriet instantly shut her mouth, and then the Mayor added before taking to the stage, "Now, if you speak while someone else is talking, your lips will fall off, and before you have a chance to scoop them off the ground, a strange hairy dog will appear and gulp them down, so tight lips kids, while daddy addresses the crowd."

With pursed shut mouths, Harriet and her little brother nodded eagerly.

A loud cheer drew eyes away from the three secretive children sitting under the willow tree towards the Mayor of Tenderville as he took to the stage. The Mayor straightened his bow tie, hitched his shoulders and stood tall. Once the cheering quietened, he cleared his throat and stepped forth to the microphone. The microphone squealed and the audience winced, then in a loud voice (not normally needed when speaking in a microphone — because that's the point of a microphone; to allow the speaker to speak normally and not have to yell their message) the Mayor said, "I'm delighted to welcome you all to the thirty-fourth celebration of Tenderville's grape and orange growing success. Unlike our neighbouring town, Onionville, where the mustard is good and the pickles are terrible." The crowd snickered and giggled, and the Mayor continued. "To open this year's festival, please put your hands together for Mr Hollingsworth who has built us a new pavilion."

The crowd applauded and cheered.

Quinton and Alan waved toffy apples in the air.

With her bubble machine, Vanessa blew enormous bubbles that took to the sky.

Megan and Mabel clapped loudly.

Lilly picked at a scab on her knee.

Herbert, Linda, Debra, Miriam, Susan, Flo and Rose stuffed their faces with battered and deep fried sausages on a stick.

As for Melissa and Shane, they crept away to ride on the dodgem cars.

Jacob, Ethan, Steven, Yonis, Jaybir, Ulas, Shawn, Mankirat, Jordan, Sehajibir, Tyrese and Hisham all went off to play soccer on the green oval, while Dean agreed to be their referee.

Benjamin, Cornelius, Stanley, Georgina, Ava, Olivia, Juliette, Ivy, Kendal, Lucia, Ruby and Remy snuck off to watch the shadow puppets, something that Archor's eyes refused to look at, and Morden and Lilac knowing that making shadow puppets required thumbs, they also pretended the puppet show didn't exist. Instead, Archor, Morden and Lilac sat on their picnic rug and shared fizzy ginger juice and sucked on oranges.

"This new pavilion is a wonderful place for all the cows, pigs and alpacas to rest when not being judged," continued the Mayor, his voice booming into the microphone.

Archor swallowed down his ginger juice and envied the animals fleetingly for having a place to rest whilst not being judged.

Then the Mayor's fingers searched for his scissors that hung from a chain from his waist coat, that also held his wallet (that had enough money for two bags of pink fairy floss for his children, a ride on the dodgem cars, and just enough left over to pay the mortgage on the small white clad cottage he and his wife had purchased on Main Street). Beside his wallet was the watch that was once his great-great-grandfathers, and a pair of silver plated scissors with his name carved in eloquent calligraphy lettering — a new gift from his wife — to cut the ribbon and announce the official opening of the new pavilion.

The crowd applauded loudly the moment the scissors snipped the ribbon in two.

Archor was fascinated by the fancy scissors, and he too cheered the cutting of the ribbon.

"Come on, Archor," said Lilac, "Let's go look around the fair."

Morden stood and Archor only followed once the Mayor's scissors had disappeared back inside his waist coat.

*   *   *

Morden, Lilac and Archor had a go at every game at the fair. They spat watermelon seeds to see how far they could shoot from their lips, they played three games in a row of tossing rings over soda bottles, they pitched balls at stacks of tin cans with crazy faces painted on them, shot air pellets at metal ducks (and did not hear a single *Ting!*). They entered the sack race and the three-legged race, they hurled horse shoes at a metal post (again, no *Ting!*), and had six attempts at guessing how many candies filled an orange crate. Towards the end of the day Morden, Lilac and Archor had just about spent all their money and played every game at the fair — but none of them had won a single thing.

There was one game left that they had not yet tried.

At the very end of the isle was a game that had no fancy stand, no fancy sign, and no fancy costumed person screaming into a microphone enticing them to play. Instead, all that was there was a little table with a rich red velvet tablecloth. On the table were three white cups and three coloured balls placed in a row in front. Behind the table was a magician in a black top hat, with a wand tucked behind his ear and his nose stuck in a book (as in, his nose wasn't actually detached from his face and stuck inside a book; he was *reading* a book!).

"Look, Lilac, a magic table," said Archor.

Morden and Lilac didn't seem as impressed by the little table, but Archor, who loved anything that was magical, saw things a little differently. "Let's play."

"Oh, Archor! You probably know all the tricks there are. There would be no fun in it."

"That is the fun, Lilac. I can outwit the magician. In fact, I could probably show him a trick or two."

"No, Archor. Leave him alone. He looks like he needs the money. Don't cheat him. Look at his horrid costume," whispered Lilac. "Your mother should make him something much, much better. Something a real magician would wear. Something with glitter sleeves and brass buttons."

"My mother won't sew magic costumes anymore, not since my father ..." Archor trailed off and it seemed at that moment the whole fair went quiet.

Lilac shifted her feet and looked uncomfortable. "Sorry, Archor."

"My mother just makes dresses now; just dresses. No more magic costumes."

"I know," said Lilac, "and very pretty dresses, too. The best in town."

Morden who stood beside them had not heard a word spoken. Instead he had spent the whole time scratching his chin and looking puzzled at the cups. "It's all to do with maths," he said, "process of elimination."

Archor who knew and understood magic well said, "Not really. It's more-"

"Maths Archor, it's all about maths. Something I'm exceptionally good at," interrupted Morden.

The magician who seemed to have ignored them up to that point snapped his book shut startling all three of them and said, "Welcome gentlemen and young lady. The cup and ball game has baffled generations for decades. Care to have a game? Are your eyes quicker than my hands? Let me double your coin, young sir."

"It's got nothing to do with the eye," said Morden, and he tossed a coin onto the velvet covered table. "What do I win?"

"What would the lady like?"

Lilac's face lit up. "The kewpie doll, the green one."

The magician smiled and put Morden's coin into his pocket.

Then the magician placed one ball under the cup and put the other two balls into Lilac's pockets. From behind the table he started to move and mix up the cups as he rattled on without taking a breath: "... quick hands, quick eyes, follow the ball and try to guess where they will be once I stop and if you guess I'll double your money is it under the right cup or the left cup or is it in the middle cup can your eyes follow the ball let's see how clever you are can you keep up are you doing your maths sir?"

"Stop!" cried Lilac. "You're making me dizzy."

The magician stopped and smiled at Morden, "Well?"

Morden swallowed, his mathematic elimination had only ended up subtracting his coin. "Hmm, the middle one. No wait! The left, yes, definitely the right. ... in the middle."

"Do you pick the middle one, young sir?"

Morden nodded and the magician slowly lifted the white cup and revealed — nothing.

"Not to worry," said Lilac.

"Young lady, would you like a guess?"

Lilac hesitated, but the temptation was too great. Lilac was also good at maths and knew it was a fifty-fifty chance, which are exceptionally good odds, (but a real mathematician who went to University would know it was 1 in 3, but Lilac was not at University yet).

"Hmm, I think the ball is under the cup on the right."

The magician lifted the white cup and three balls rolled out. "Check your pockets, madam."

Lilac slipped her hands inside her pockets to find them both empty. The two balls the magician had placed in her pockets only moments earlier had indeed disappeared. Lilac clapped and squealed delighted. Archor laughed, but Morden shrugged, unimpressed and indifferent to the result. "Come on, let's go."

"Wait." Archor had played the magic three-cup ball game many times before and had developed an understanding for the trick behind the magic. He knew he could outwit the magician and win Morden's money back.

"Let me try," said Archor.

But the magician saw something in Archor and knew he wasn't playing with an ordinary kid. The magician said, "Instead of you playing my game of the magic three cups, what if you show me a magic trick?"

"What would be the point?"

"If you show me a trick that is impressive, I'll give the lady the little green doll. If I show you a trick that you cannot tell me how it's done, then you owe me ..." the magician hesitated and the three held their breath waiting for him to finish, "... you owe me a story."

"A story? What kind of story?" asked Archor.

"Your story."

The three children laughed.

It was, indeed, a strange request.

Archor accepted, after all, what harm is in telling a story? "Your hat, if you will."

The magician gave Archor his top hat and wand. Archor pattered the top hat down hard on his head and placed the three white cups in a row upside down. He placed one ball on top of the middle cup and stacked the other two cups on top. He tapped his wand and when he lifted all three cups at once, there was a ball underneath the stack. It appeared that the ball had penetrated through the cup.

"Tah-dah!"

Lilac laughed, but Morden's cheeks were becoming hot and his fists were curling up into two tight balls of their own, "Okay, that's enough, we all know you can do magic."

"But I'm not done," said Archor.

The magician smiled. "I like your magic. I know this trick and it is indeed clever. I will let the girl have her doll."

The magician handed Lilac the little green kewpie doll and Lilac hugged Archor carelessly and awkwardly and a little too hard that it bent and squashed his ear and made the top hat fall off his head.

"Let's see if Archor can see how your magic trick is done," said Morden.

"Oh, it's not *my* magic trick," said the magician, "it's hers."

Both Archor and Morden looked at Lilac, who blushed.

"Not her, *her.*"

Over Lilac's shoulder was a dark royal blue tent.

"I'm talking about the fortune teller. The Mystic le Fay. This is a different type of magic altogether."

Archor swallowed. He handed back the magician his hat and wand, and then slowly slipped his hands into his pockets, so no one could see his eight fingers tremble.

"Well? I don't know what you two are waiting for. I'm going to see what she has to say about my fortune." Morden began to trudge up the hill and Lilac and Archor quickly followed.

At the top of the hill Morden, Lilac and Archor stood a short, comfortable distance from The Mystic le Fay's tent. It was a rich royal blue tapestry. If you looked closely, you could see pictures of greyhounds, forest trees and hunters on horseback. The whole tent was trimmed in gold with tassels. After some hesitation the three inched a little closer, and as they did a long pale slender arm popped out of the opening flap of the tent. Its long spidery fingers, with dark red painted nails curled and beckoned them to enter. The pointer finger curled again and again like a tiny red ocean wave.

"You go first," said Lilac with a quiver in her voice. She pushed Archor towards the opening flap.

"I'll go first," said Morden, and he stepped out from behind them and instantly disappeared inside the tent.

Lilac gripped Archor's elbow and took a deep breath. This was a strange magic that none of them could explain, a different type of magic; one they felt they should not be playing with.

"It's okay," said Archor, "I'll look after you."

"I know," answered Lilac.

They waited a long time in silence until the slender pale arm appeared again through the tent flap, and the pointer finger with its glossy long red nail curled again like the hypnotic rolling of ocean waves.

Archor went to step forward, but Lilac held him back by the elbow. "Ladies before gentleman, Archor. Let me go next."

"It's okay, I'll go."

"Please, let me. While I still have the nerve." And Lilac disappeared through the flap of the tent.

The wait was excruciating. Archor's patience was pushed to its limit. The seconds felt like minutes, and the minutes felt like hours. His mind filled with hundreds of thoughts, and most of them horrible. He wondered what was happening to his friends, and he was frightened of what may be said. What would the mystic see? But most of all, Archor felt more than ever before, ashamed of his missing thumbs.

At last, the pale slender arm popped out from the tent flap, only the curling finger didn't roll and entice, it pointed straight at Archor, and then in a flash it disappeared back inside the tent. Archor presumed that meant for him to enter, and he peeled back the tent flap and stepped inside.

Archor looked around the small room and gasped. The beauty of it took his breath. Inside the colours were rich and vibrant. Hundreds of cushions scattered the floor. Wind chimes of many descriptions and sizes hung from the pitch in the tents roof. Little golden pots smoked and smelt of lavender and rose and vanilla. It was a smell that, much later in life, he would come to know as *Dragon's blood*.

But what was even more beautiful than the inside of the tent, was the Mystic le Fay herself.

"Sit, boy."

Her voice sounded like the song of a bellbird and her eyes resembled the eyes on a peacock's tail, a deep blue centre surrounded by a turquoise green haze that seemed to reflect a golden hue. Her lips looked like they were pasted in blood, and her skin looked even paler against her black inky hair and brows. Archor had lost his voice and stared hypnotised by her radiance.

"Please, sit. You will be more comfortable."

Archor could hardly feel his legs and thought they may buckle beneath him and he'd fall face first to the floor (which made him think, maybe that was why there were so many cushions on the floor), but somehow he managed to sit.

Next to the mystic was a tall ornamental hollow glass stand. It had a vase at the bottom, carved by an ancient Indian glass craftsman. It had an apple on top, and foil over the apple with holes punched in it. On top of the foil sat red hot coals. The mystic took a long pipe that was attached to the glass stand and sucked. She blew out a wad of smoke that smelt like apple, coconut and mint.

"It's called an Arguily," she said to Archer. "It is smoked in exotic locations like Turkey, India and China."

"I've never left Tenderville. How far to India?"

"Oceans away," laughed the mystic. "The Arguily teaches patience and tolerance and above all, appreciation for good company. It helps one to focus."

Archor sat tall and paid closer attention to the mystic, fearful that she might just shove the pipe into his mouth if he didn't. Instead she laid the mouth piece of the pipe down on her lap and asked, "May I have your hand, please?"

"Hand?"

"Your palm."

"Palm? You read palms?" Archor was more afraid than embarrassed to show her his hands. "Not the crystal ball? Or a pack of cards?"

"I don't do crystals or tarots. I read palms. If you give me your left hand, I will tell you the life you were born to have. If you give me your right hand, I can tell you what you will do with this life."

Archor slipped his hands from his pockets and looked at them both. He then laid one palm down in front of the mystic. She did not flinch or blink, or recoil from the image of a thumbless hand. Nor did she show any signs of even noticing Archor's missing thumb. Instead, she picked up his hand in both of hers and gently ran her finger down the smooth edge where Archor's thumb should have grown. His hand was perfect, perfectly thumbless. She nursed his hand as though it was precious and delicate. She turned it over, ran her finger across the tiny lines on his palm and smiled and spoke in her song bird voice,

"A life without thumbs will bring purity, honesty, love and true friendship."

Archor sat gazing at The Mystic le Fay until he realised she had nothing else to say. "Is that it?"

"Yes. That is all. You can slip out the back of the tent and return to your friends."

Dumfounded, Archor slipped his hand away from the mystic and stood. He could still feel her touch and warmth where her fingers followed the lines on his palm. He had to force his eyes away from hers and then he left without a word, exiting through the back flap of her tent.

Morden and Lilac had waited beside the magician for Archor to return. They were afraid he would be upset and angry by the reading. They had seen Archor flare-up and scorn those that drew attention to his missing thumbs, then watch him spend the days that followed stewing on the topic until they convinced him to let it go. So, when Archor appeared calm and happy, they were both confused.

"Well?" asked the magician, "What is your story?"

Archor replied, "She told me that a life without thumbs will bring purity, honesty, love and true friendship."

Morden and Lilac looked at each other.

"Hmm, your friends were told something different," said the magician.

Archor could tell by the look on Lilac's face that he may not like to hear what they had been told, but still, he asked, "What did she tell you?"

Morden's fists finally uncurled from the tight balls they had been in, his shoulders relaxed and he oddly felt happy as he said, "We were told a life without thumbs will sink miserably in your heart at the truth of being left thumbless."

"You three have been told different fortunes," said the magician.

Archor felt his cheeks burn, while Morden felt his cheeks relax. Archor knew that because he had no thumbs the mystic had taken pity on him and he had been lied too.

"That's where the trick is, in the lie," said Archor to the magician. "You owe my friend his coin." Archor turned on his heels and stormed off towards home, brewing and stewing, and when he thought no one could see him, he let the tears fall from the bottom of his eyelids and roll down his cheeks.

"Archor!" called Lilac, but Archor did not stop.

Archor's stomach churned and his mind could not let the words go. What Archor didn't know at the time was that the fortune teller was correct in all their readings. Archor had just lost his faith and let the words become negative and reflective of him. And in the years to come it would be difficult for him to know if this moment started his new destination, or was the fortune teller's prediction of his destiny correct all along?

*   *   *

That night Archor hid under his blankets with a torch, a pencil and pad of paper.

What epiphany Archor had is none of our business and not for us to see. But he did scribble something in 2B pencil, which looked oddly like a glove.

But not being one who wants to be guilty of gossip, I will simply say, it is not for us to judge or condemn a person for their feelings and life experiences — alas, it is easier and kind to say, no one will ever know what he drew, and it is none of our business (some of the best ideas in the world come into people's imaginations late at night, so you should never make fun or disturb them.)

Let's leave Archor in peace.

Archor at age eleven and a half

Archor was now a little older. He was also a little taller, and a little smarter.

Archor grabbed his sneakers from the cupboard under the stairs and sat on the bottom step to put his shoes on. As he tied his laces into large loops he called, "See you, Mum. I'm off now," and just as Archor was about to race out the front door to meet up with Morden and Lilac, his mother stepped in front of him, blocking the doorway and his speedy exit.

"What's the rush?" asked Mrs Chatelaine, picking tiny coloured cotton threads off Archor's shirt.

These small off-cuts of cotton thread were found all over the Chatelaine's home. If a person visited and sat on the lounge, Mrs Chatelaine would give them a cup of tea and slice of homemade date loaf, and they would leave with a full tummy and pink and yellow cotton threads stuck to the seat of their pants.

If a visitor sat at the kitchen table, Mrs Chatelaine would give them a mug of coffee and melted cheese on crusty bread. They would leave with a full tummy and blue, orange and green cotton threads stuck to their elbow. If Morden or Lilac lolled the afternoon on Archor's bed they would leave hungry, and have black and red cotton threads stuck to their tummy.

These little cotton threads that were snipped off here and there, always found a way to stick and cling to the Chatelaine's guests and let everyone in Tenderville know whose house they had returned from. All the ladies in Tenderville could never understand how their husbands knew they were thinking about purchasing a new dress, but the secret was that their husbands noticed these delicate threads of coloured cotton from where Mrs Chatelaine had draped fabric over their wives shoulders, or asked them to stay for a cup of tea or coffee.

So as Mrs Chatelaine picked at the tiny threads stuck to Archor's shirt she said, "Now Archor, before you race off, remember your manners."

"Yes, Mum."

"I mean it Archor. You will go a long way in life with good manners and a kind heart."

Archor rolled his eyes.

"It's true. A kind word warms the heart, a cold word closes it."

"I know, I know, it's better to close your ears to negativity, than to close your heart."

"Or, how about this one Archor. Don't use a person who has lived a life of hardship to be your yard stick to measure your own good fortune. Use the noble man's life as your yard stick. It is more admirable to live up to something, than to look down upon something."

"Or how about this one Mum. It is better to allow your child to discover his own lessons, and eat his breakfast in peace, rather than inflict confusion and indigestion."

"Hmm. Sit down, Archor. I want to tell you a little story."

Archor had not only grown taller by the age of eleven and a half, he had also grown much smarter, and he knew the sooner he sat down and let his mother tell her story, the sooner he would get out the front door and meet up with his friends. Archor also knew a *little* story was *not* the same as a *short* story.

The trick was;

1. Keep quiet; don't interrupt or the story will go longer.

2. Smile; a bored or disinterested face will make the story go into more detail.

3. Pretend to understand; if you look like you have no idea what the point of the story is, you will only be told another one (often longer than the first).

4. Be thankful; otherwise you will have the story explained in excruciating detail back to you with the point and all the lessons you missed in it re-explained, until you are *more than* thankful.

5. Praise the story teller; or the story teller will tell you how lucky you are to have a story teller and not an annoying mother who would otherwise just give you the same lesson in a dull and uninteresting way, and then proceed to tell the lesson *again* in a dull and uninteresting way.

"It's just a little story Archor, it won't take long, but its importance will last much longer than its telling."

Archor smiled and sat back down on the bottom step. "Tell me your little story, Mum."

A Little Story

Once upon a time there was a little old lady, who lived in a small village. The village was a long way from the city — so far — the villagers had to collect their water from a nearby river. The whole village used this water to drink; boil their vegetables; water their flowers; and bathe their children (and themselves).

Every morning the women would meet by the river and chatter while collecting buckets of water. In winter, they had to crack through the thin ice on the surface before lowering and submerging their buckets. In summer, they'd splash the water about with their toes to cool their feet in the running stream, before filling up their buckets. Whenever the little old lady arrived to fill her bucket, the women would say hello. The little old lady never replied.

The women would snicker and say, "How rude!"

"She speaks to nobody."

"Just ignore her, girls."

"Too good to speak to the likes of us!"

The little old lady would fill her bucket and return home.

As the years crept by the water level of the river lowered, until one year the water level was so low that it hardly trickled over the pebbles. Where water collected in pools it smelled and had turned a sickly orange colour that was undrinkable. What little fresh water remained, the villagers had agreed to be extra careful with.

"No more wasting water."

"No more splashing."

"Water only the vegetables and not your flowers."

"Limit your baths."

The little old lady however, chose not to bath altogether. She only drank the water sparingly from her bucket and with her unused bathing ration, she made mud cakes.

"Mud cakes?"

"Has she lost her mind?"

"Mud cakes, indeed!"

"Look at her, digging up the ground and making those ridiculous mud pies."

"Waste of water!"

"And look at how dirty she is."

"She should use her water to bathe!"

For more than a month, the little old lady continued to only drink her water sparingly; she never bathed; she ate raw vegetables; she dug her hole deeper; and stacked her mud pies higher.

One day the river ran dry. The women of the small village were fearful — and furious.

"We are out of water!"

"All this time she has been wasting her water, making mud cakes."

"We have children to feed."

"She just digs and digs and with the left over water makes mud pies!"

"Silly old woman!"

"No," said one of the smaller children. "She's not wasting water. She is digging a well and making the walls strong with her mud bricks."

The women of the village looked at the boy for a moment, and then they started to laugh.

"She'll never find water down there."

"She'll never dig deep enough."

"Impossible."

"That underground spring is too deep."

"The task is too hard."

"She won't succeed."

The child felt sorry for the little old lady. He poured the last drops of water from his bucket into a small cup and took it to her. The child leant over the mud brick wall and looked down into the well. "Excuse me," said the boy. His voice echoed and bounced off the walls of the well.

"Yes?" came a reply from the bottom of the well.

Everyone gasped. The little old lady had never spoken before.

"Would you like a cup of my water?"

"No, thank you," came the reply. "I think I have found some of my own. Would you prefer a bucket of mine?"

"Yes, please," answered the boy.

"Bring your bucket and tell the villagers to bring theirs."

The little old lady shared the water from her well with the whole village.

When the child asked the little old lady why she didn't feel hurt or resentful for the way the other women had spoken to her, or why she didn't feel discouraged when they didn't believe she could build a well, it turned out the little old lady was deaf.

"But you can hear me now," said the child.

"Yes, I can," said the little old lady. "The funnel-shaped walls of the well have collected the sound waves and led them to my ear. You see, inside the well the voice is strengthened and makes for better hearing. Outside the well, my hearing is not so good."

Not only was the village saved with its own water supply, it is said that many years later the child who offered to share his water with the little old lady, grew up to invent the very first hearing trumpet.

Archor smiled and said, "That was such an enjoyable story, Mum. I really enjoyed and understood all of it. A great moral, indeed. Thank you for telling it. Can I please go now?"

"Before you rush off to play, I have just one more thing Archor, follow me." Mrs Chatelaine left for the lounge room and Archor, with his teeth firmly clenched and his eyes burning holes up at the ceiling, reluctantly followed his mother into the lounge room.

By the dusty bay window, Mrs Chatelaine sat down at her sewing machine. She pressed the wrought iron peddle with her foot and spun a small wheel attached to the side of the machine with her hand. The needle of the sewing machine began to go up and down, up and down, faster and faster, and the noise of the machine grew louder, and louder, until all of the sudden she took her foot off the peddle and grabbed tight to the wheel with both hands and stopped the machine instantly. She used her teeth to snap the cotton thread and free the garment from the machine.

"Here, Archor. I made these for you," and Mrs Chatelaine handed Archor a pair of skin coloured gloves for his four fingers to slide into, and where his thumbs should be, his mother had made a padded thumb. They looked like perfect hands.

"Thank you, Mum."

Archor hugged his mother for a very long time.

The Rule of Thumbs

It should be noted, that while mothers will do anything for their sons to make life more pleasant, they don't have to like it or agree with it. It should also be noted that Mrs Chatelaine did not like Archor's idea of fake thumb gloves at all. But eventually she was worn down by Archor's persistence and reluctance to let the topic go, so as Archor's hands grew, or the gloves became too difficult to clean, Mrs Chatelaine would make Archor a new pair of four finger gloves and stuffed the thumbs of the glove with wadding and present them to him. They were almost perfect. Only a very keen eye would have noticed that it was not skin, but tight fitting skin-coloured gloves on Archor's hands. Mrs Chatelaine's sewing skills were indeed, exceptional. And for months leading up to the next festival, the people of Tenderville had learnt to either ignore or accept Archor's pretend thumbs and gloved hands.

The 37th Annual Orange
and Grape Festival

Three years had gone by since Morden, Lilac and Archor had entered the royal blue tent of the Mystic le Fay. At every festival following that year, the mystic was nowhere to be seen. She had been forgotten long ago.

A lot had happened to the three friends since then; they had all grown taller; they had lost their baby teeth and grown their adult teeth; Lilac had grown her hair; and they had grown much closer as friends; as you do when time travels alongside you. And Archor had finally grown to live with his thumbless hands. Perhaps that's not quite the right way of looking at things. Archor had found another way to live *without* his thumbs, and that was to live *with* thumbs, by wearing the skin-coloured gloves his mother made for him.

At the 37th annual Orange and Grape Festival (Archor with his gloved hands) and the rest of Tenderville applauded with all their fingers and thumbs when the town's Mayor once again took to the stage and opened the festival.

Over the years not only had Morden, Lilac and Archor's friendship grown, so had the festival. Apart from the fairy floss machine, toffee apples, lemonade, street parade with stilt walkers, clowns and marching band, each year the festival boasted something new. The town now had a rollercoaster ride, a loop-the-loop and for the first time a circus had come to town to entertain Tenderville. They had put up an enormous red and white striped tent and promised a show beyond the town's imagination.

"It will be the magic show of all magic shows," the Mayor said, a little too loudly into the squeaky microphone.

The big top was the talk of the town and the most anticipated event that evening. Nearly everyone in town had a ticket, and those that didn't, pouted.

As the Mayor stood on the stage with his wife by his side and his five children, aged nine, seven, three and twins in a pram all watching from the side, everyone's eyes was on the enormous tent behind him. Nobody had seen the inside and everyone was too busy whispering about what it would be like in there, instead of listening to the Mayors long, drawn out speech.

"Hmm," the Mayor sighed, noticing his own children growing tied of his prattling. "Now Harriet, if I see you kick your brother one more time, I'll confiscate your legs!" said the Mayor over his shoulder. His daughter snapped her heels together and stood perfectly still as the Mayor continued his praise for the circus and asked all the town folk of Tenderville to make their visiting guests feel most welcome.

Apart from the circus being something very different, Archor also noticed that this was the first year that Mr Hollingsworth was not thanked for making another contribution. In the past he had made picnic benches, a pavilion, paddle boats and a wharf for kids to jump off into the lake and swim with the trout. But Mr Hollingsworth did not look sad, or disappointed, in fact he looked happy — very happy. Archor could not be sure from where he was sitting, but he was almost certain that Mr Hollingsworth had a little yellow cotton thread clinging to the seat of his pants.

On stage the Mayor's fingers searched for his scissors that hung from the chain from his waist coat, that also held his wallet (that had enough money for five battered sausages on a stick, three bags of fairy floss, and just enough left over to put a down payment on an extension on his cottage that would add an extra bedroom and give his wife and himself a little more breathing space in their home on Main Street). Beside his wallet was the watch that was once his great-great-grandfather's, and a pair of gold plated scissors with a blue stone at the pivoting point and the names of all five children carved in eloquent calligraphy lettering — a new gift from his wife — to cut the ribbon and announce the official opening. And that's exactly what he did — in one snip — except when the Mayor tucked the scissors back inside his coat jacket he forgot to close them fully, and only people in Eastern Europe countries know the superstition that leaving scissors open causes fights and disagreements within a household. But the Mayor of Tenderville was not from Eastern Europe or superstitious, and that evening he fought with his children about the state of their bedrooms, and then his wife fought with him about the state of his temper. It cost the Mayor six apologies; one pony ride; two bedtime stories; three hugs; one Eskimo kiss; one game of thumb wars and a sincere promise that it wouldn't happen again. The Mayor learnt, sometimes you don't need to yell your demands, you should try and ask politely first. Yelling is only after the fifth attempt to get a child to pick up their toys, and even then it's not a very nice thing to do. But parents are human, and just like a grizzly bear, when tied, they roar!

The town of Tenderville applauded and whooped, delighted with the opening ceremony and then they began to disperse and join friends and family on rides and share the food inside their baskets, catch up with old stories and most important, enjoyed their friendships with one another.

*   *   *

In the late afternoon Archor and Lilac sat lazily by the river, watching paddleboats drift by. They were worn out from the big slide and carousel. They had eaten all the goodies in their show-bag (so they had nothing left for when they got home), they were full of ice-cream and pie and now they just wanted to loll on the grass and do nothing but watch the coloured paddleboat wheels rotate pastel shades as they pass them by.

Lilac sighed and lay on her back. She smiled up at the sky, with her eyes that were the colour of violets. She squinted against the warm sun as she snuggled deeper into the thick wild grass, hidden amongst the zoysia, a pretty grass flower, and daffodils.

Archor was by her side, but the two could not see each other, both buried deep and concealed by the wall of tall wild green grass between them. The wind swept over them, but didn't touch their face and they could smell the strong sent of daffodils. The flowers yellow trumpets were silent as the two chatted about things only they could speak of.

"Your father was once a great magician. Magical in every way," said Lilac.

"Hmm," replied Archor.

"Do you still have his wand?"

"Yes," said Archor, "It still has my teeth marks where I chewed on it as a baby."

"That's special."

"Maybe," said Archor. "But all magic can be explained, eventually. You just have to work out how they do the trick."

"Do you think if you can uncover all magic tricks that that would make your father real? And not mystical?" asked Lilac.

Archor rolled to his side, and while he could not see Lilac behind the grass and daffodil stems, he knew she was there. "My father was great. But one day his magic all went wrong. He found another type of magic that he couldn't explain."

"What type of magic?" asked Lilac.

"My mother won't say, but it's the reason why it's just the two of us now. Just Mum and me. My mother believes I'm magical. But I've learnt all the tricks behind magic, and I know that there is no such thing. It's a gimmick, an illusion, and while it's fun and entertaining, there is always a trick."

Lilac pushed the grass aside between them and saw Archor's face only an inch from hers. She leant forward and kissed Archor on the cheek and asked, "Is there magic in that? Or am I a gimmick, Archor?"

And before Archor could answer, Lilac had run off down to the wharf and the paddle boats, all that was left was the grass imprint where she had laid and Archor was sure the daffodils had sounded their trumpets and the wind was laughing at him.

"That was the magic that stole my father, the magic of another woman," said Archor to no one, because there was no longer anyone left to listen.

*   *   *

That night as Archor arrived at the big top, the wind playfully tickled his nose and cheeks. It filled his nostrils with the sweetness in the air and tricked him into thinking the evening had favoured him. Archor thought it was a pleasant night, but he had no idea the weather was about to change. Inside the tent Archor, Morden and Lilac were warmly greeted by the circus ushers and shown to their seats. As Archor sat he had no idea that sometimes what we see on stage is nothing like what is happening back-stage.

Under the brilliant candy striped canopy the audience sat in anticipation looking up at the stage and waited for the show to start, while back stage, behind the black curtain, down at the end of the dark corridor, between the white ponies and the lions, the Ringmaster twisted the leather whip in his hand and said to the magician, "Your magic act is an artless-weedy-beetle-headed serving of maggot-pie and bull's pizzel! Not even a pig-nut inside a pigeon-egg would come out of its shell to watch it."

The magician scratched his head and looked confused, "Pardon?"

"Your act is terrible! And tonight, if it's not any better, I'm gonna have to leave you behind in this town."

"But I've been with this circus for–"

"I don't care!"

"But I've given it my everything–"

"I don't care!"

The magician's face went pale. He was concerned for his future and fretful for his dreams, "But, but, I'm a magician, it's all I know how to do? It's all I can do. Where will I go?"

"You can always stay in Tenderville and pick fruit!" huffed the Ringmaster.

"What's magical about that?"

"Nothing! So tonight I don't want to see a droning-dankish-dizzy-eyed-bat-fouling-clay-brained-onion-eyed-frothy-gleeking-loggerheaded-puking-puny-ruttish-boil-brained-flap-mouthed-fool-born-plume-plucked-malt-worm-cod-fish-bladder-pressing-barnacle performance!"

"Pardon?"

"Don't make any mistakes!"

"Oh, okay ... " and in that very instant, the magician lost his enthusiasm for all things magical. The years that he had honed his skills, practiced and perfected his craft, dedicated his life to his art, his passion, his love, his dream of being a great magician vanished! All because the cost of failure was too great, too humiliating, and too painful.

Oh, the irony of it; something he had loved his whole life, would end up costing him everything, and in that instant, the magician started to accept the idea that maybe he would be picking oranges and crushing grapes for the rest of his life.

And he took comfort in the darkness, because no one could see him weep for the love of magic that had left him, for the dream of being great that he had lost and for the emptiness he felt. His passion had vanished.

*   *   *

It was the first time Archor had ever been or seen inside a theatre. It was the most exciting thing he had ever experienced. There was a great sense of something special about it, like he had always belonged to it. Like a pair of shoes that are brand new, but you feel like you have worn them forever. Archor just knew he had stepped into something that had captured his imagination and heart. Never before had he truly felt like he belonged to something, but there inside the tent's enormous dome, he knew that was where he belonged.

As the circus band started to play and the lights lit up the stage, Archor watched and instantly felt a great love for the stage, a great envy for the performers. He wanted to jump up on stage and be right beside them. It was because it was there in that theatre, in that moment in the darkness he was just like everyone else. He could watch the show, be free to get swept away with the entertainment on stage, and what he realised was, you don't need thumbs to applaud. You don't need thumbs to enjoy a theatrical performance. And he truly believed in his heart, he wouldn't need thumbs to be a part of it.

Under the big top, together the audience and the performers were all one in the darkness.

Lilac sat on the hard bench seat between Archor and Morden and stuffed hot buttery popcorn into her mouth. She smiled and giggled and popcorn sprinkled her lap, which only made her laugh more. In the darkness, Lilac could relax and be herself. She knew no one would be staring at her violet eyes, or the golden threads of her hair that captured the sunlight, her plump blueberry lips and thin neck. In the darkness she was just a shadow, just a dark outline and nothing special to look at.

Morden loved the darkness because it allowed him to feel Lilacs shoulder brush against his without her even knowing she had connected with him. His arm would tingle and his mouth would go dry and Morden would wish he could reach out his hand and hold hers. Perhaps the darkness would let him. Morden also felt more relaxed in the dark, because he didn't need to look at Archor's hideous gloved hands and their ridiculous fake thumbs. Those gloves made Morden squirm. It made him frown and wish all of Archor was like his thumbs — not there. Morden liked the darkness, because no one could see the contempt he had for Archor's gloved hands, or the great desire he had to hold Lilacs whole and perfect hand.

*   *   *

On stage, to your left and to your right side are long black curtains. These curtains are called the wings.

It's a place where the performer stands before stepping out on stage. The curtains hide the performer from the audience, sometimes the audience doesn't even know the performer is there — but the performer always knows the audience is there, they can feel the audience's presence.

And here is a strange thing, the more you perform, the more you can feel what your audience is like, before you even see them, before you have even stepped out on stage, you can tell if the audience is going to like you, or you are going to have to work really hard to win them over. Some actors call it a gift, some say it comes with the experience of many years of walking the stage floorboards, but the performer can always feel the mood of the audience before they begin (and only the great performers know they are capable of changing that mood).

In the wings, performers also do strange things. Some pray; some madly flick through the script and look like they are going to their doom; some mouth the words with no sound; some hum in their heads; some wiggle their fingers and breathe in deeply; some are excited; some are calm; and some look stiff as a dodo, like someone has just struck them over the head with a frying pan.

Lots of people don't even know the performer is doing this, because often it is dark in the wings between those thick black curtains, and in that space between the stage and backstage, it is the one place a performer can truly be alone with themself.

Every night the magician had always stood in the wings and felt that he could fly. He thought that was why they called it the wings; because he could feel the upward lift, the encouragement to step out, step up and move forward into the spotlight.

Every night, he felt this was the place he was meant to be. But now, in the darkness, he couldn't seem to feel the audience, instead he only heard their rustling feet, the noisy chewing of food and low murmuring. His swallowed and a zillion butter flies filled the emptiness in his stomach. His throat was dry, and he felt he had forgotten all his tricks. He could hear the sound of his heart thump in his ears and feel it in his chest.

He wanted the curtain wings to wrap around him and protect him. He couldn't seem to remember any of his routine. He could only remember the sound of the Ringmasters voice yelling, "no mistakes, you goatish-toad-spotted-whey-face-flap-dragon!"

In the darkness the magician closed his eyes and wished he could be anywhere, but there. The magic had left him and he felt he could no longer fly.

*   *   *

But not everything bad happens in the darkness. Sometimes things quite special happen in the dark. Like worms that help improve the soil that makes your vegetables grow, and mushrooms like the dark, and bats enjoy a good fly around in the dark. You grow taller whilst asleep and you do most of that in the dark.

Archor's mother arrived in the dark. She slipped in through the back door and sat beside Mr Hollingsworth in the back row. In the dark the two smiled, and while they could not see each other's face, they still knew they had made each other smile. See, even a smile can be felt in the dark.

The magician now stood centre stage in the spotlight. The sequence of his costume glittered and the colours looked brilliant and vibrant, but the magician did not feel the same. You see, in the spotlight the light is so intense that you can't see the faces of the audience; you are almost blinded by the strength of light that has washed over you. Oh, you know the audience is there, you can hear them, feel them, but the light stops you from seeing them. The light is also very warm, and after a while, you begin to sweat. It starts in your hair line, and then you feel moist behind your ears, your lip is next, and then your neck. Before you know it, you look drenched and your face begins to flush, and unless you are comfortable up there, you start to want to go to the toilet. This was how the magician was feeling.

What he should have done was take some very slow deep breaths, swallowed and wiggled his fingers and toes, smiled and stopped any negative thoughts. And he would have, if it were not for the Ringmaster in the wings hissing, "Keep going, do another trick, a better trick this time. Do something to wow the audience!"

The magic show was not going well at all. The magician cupped his hand over his forehead to block out the spotlight so he could see into the audience.

"A volunteer, if you please," called the magician.

Why on earth he wanted to drag anyone into his show, no one will ever know, but at that moment Archor saw his big opportunity and his hand raised in a flash.

The magician saw the spirit and enthusiasm in Archor's face, and sensed something magical about him and he agreed for Archor to take to the stage alongside him.

Archor raced up onto the stage. He did not feel nervous in the spotlight. The heat from the lights warmed his face, and although he couldn't see the crowd, or his friends, there was an element of mystery about performing in front of an invisible wall that separated the light from the darkness. He did squint his eyes and searched for Lilac, but she was lost behind the forth invisible wall and was in a sea of darkness. (This was the queue for the magician to look after his guest, give some encouraging words and make him feel comfortable, but because the magician was under so much pressure, he forgot all about Archor and focused only on his next trick. Besides, Archor needed no encouragement).

"For my next trick I will make these coloured handkerchiefs disappear from my guest's hands."

The magician showed the audience two handkerchiefs, one blue and one green, "Can you clench both your fists sir?"

Archor clenched his fists tight and the magician stuffed the silk material down through the tight circular opening that Archor's curled fingers made.

"On the count of three I will tap my volunteer's hands and make the handkerchiefs inside disappear. One, two, three!"

The magician tapped Archor's hands, "Now can you please raise your hands up into the air and slowly open them, showing your palms to the audience."

Archor held up his hands and slowly opened them, not only were the coloured silk handkerchiefs missing, so was his thumbs! The magician had accidently removed the silk handkerchiefs and Archor's gloves.

The magician gasped, but quickly beamed a forced smile at the audience to cover up the catastrophe of his mistake and said, "Tah-dah!"

The poor magician turned back at Archor horrified, but at the same time he also thought he had had a moment of greatness beyond his wildest expectations. A moment of unexplained genius. He turned back to the audience, determined to claim his applause for the wonder he had just performed (although he had no idea how he did it). "Tah-dah!" he called again and bowed.

"Bravo! Bravo!" cried the Ringmaster coming out onto the stage. "Missing thumbs, a great illusion, indeed! Bravo! Bravo! Our finest magician any circus has to offer."

The audience however knew Archor Chatelaine, and they knew he never had thumbs in the first place and that the magician's magic had gone wrong. The magician had no idea that by accident he removed the coloured silk handkerchiefs and Archor's special 'thumb' gloves. The audience roared with laughter, and the Ringmaster thought this was a good thing so he also applauded and laughed, calling "Magnificent! Magnificent!" which only made everyone laugh harder.

Archor grabbed the wrist of the magician and reached inside his sleeve and snatched back the skin coloured gloves. He gave the magician a look of great scorn, and then humiliated, Archor fled the stage.

Mrs Chatelaine cupped her hands over her face and sobbed. For the second time in her life she was responsible for Archor losing his thumbs. If only she hadn't made those ridiculous gloves.

*   *   *

As Archor raced across the fairground paddock in the distance he saw the familiar blue tapestry of a tent, it was the fortune teller, the Mystic le Fay. Archor hesitated, but then turned back and followed the track down to where the paddle wheelers were tied to the wharf. By the river Archor cupped his hands and hid them under his shirt. His love for the theatre disappeared, like a bubble that had been popped, his inspiration and enthusiasm for magic tricks vanished. He had been humiliated out of the thing he felt most passionate about and now he was left with an empty feeling. Archor had felt this before, and he knew of the emptiness felt when people took away the things you loved.

Archor could not quash his feeling of anger. He followed the river's edge until he ended up behind the new building that was soon to be the tunnel-of-love. Mr Hollingsworth was putting the final touches on the boats that would float through the tunnel and eventually float out onto the river. Archor grunted. He felt it was just an excuse for couples to kiss in the dark and not be seen. For people to hold each other's hands. It was a tunnel-of-deceit, that's what it was, people hiding their true feelings from the outside world.

In his rage, Archor grabbed a carpenter's pencil that belonged to Mr Hollingsworth and the plans for the new ride. With the pencil clutched tightly in his fist he began to scribble on the back of the plans for the tunnel-of-love. Only it wasn't childish scribble, Archor started to make a list. It was a list of all the things the children in town would no longer be able to do, if they lost their thumbs.

The List

Cecily, Prudence, Sarah & William	No longer will they mould doe
MaryAnn, Thomas, Jessica, Katie & Beatrice	Will close the piano lid
Reginald, Francis, Balunn, Gladys & Alfred	Will put down a hammer
Calleen, Lisa, Edmundo, Floyd & Flynn	Stop playing football
Elizabeth, Jehu & Jeoffroi	Stop sucking their thumbs
Robert, Nidra, Drake & Dara	Can't finish their cubby house
Wallace, Yarran & Kedric	Flies will now all keep their wings and be annoying
Susannah, Trudy, Peter, Jacinta & Faramond	Stop cooking cookies

Henry, Damiano, Samuel, Nerys & Charlotte	Will no longer decorate cakes
Ellen & Yasmin	Can no longer plait each other's hair
Heath, Jacquetta, Vanice, Barney & Chuang	Can now leave insects alone
Timothy, Nadine, Pat & Sean	Can't help mum hang out the washing
Wirrin, Lincon, Bazel, Scott & Rose	No longer enjoy playing with clay
Stuart, Mariel, Jecinta, Lara & Coral	Will give up on poetry
Murray, Tor, Chu & Deborah,	Will stop playing music
Sally, Patrick, Beau & Democritus	Will say goodbye to buttons
Baradine & Tallis	Will no longer pen a famous novel
Frederick	Father will stop selling shoes with shoe laces
Bridget, Renee & Sheldon	Can no longer paint their toe nails
Orion, Rowan, Rosie & Dal	Quit baseball, and never climb a mountain
Percy, Opal, Dawud, Olivia & Phoebe	Stop painting and colouring
Wendy, Susan & Sabrina	No more will sew
Anthony, Dako, Judah & Patience	Will lose interest growing vegetables in the garden

Kevin, Wilga, Nicholas & Alvan	No longer do archery, or wash windows
Quinton, Alan, Vanessa, Megan & Mabel	Never build another house of cards
Herbert, Linda, Rose, Melissa & Stanley	Toss away their skipping ropes
Benjamin, Cornelius, Ivy, Bertha, & Joshua	Struggle holding a book and give up
Walter, Rebecca, Esther & Kay	Never play thumb wars again
Morden and Lilac	Will never be able to hold each other's hand

*   *   *

Lilac searched the whole fair ground for Archor, calling out for him, but she did not hear him return the call. Defeated, in the end Lilac turned and walked home alone. The whole time she couldn't help wondering if he was alright, and wishing she could hold his hand. On the back of her sleeve she wiped her tears away from her violet eyes.

*   *   *

Archor looked down at the words he wrote. He felt ashamed, hardly able to read them out aloud. Before anyone could catch him with it, he stuffed the list down the back seat of one of the love-boats Mr Hollingsworth was still building. Archor composed himself and made his way home.

But that night, the bitterness would not seem to leave Archor. He paced the house, he picked up the cotton reels and pulled long strands of thread snapping them off cotton reels, all because his mother had told him, "like the cotton on a reel, my love for you is endless, it just keeps winding on and on."

But Archor knew better. He knew love didn't last forever, look at his mother and father, look at his passion and love for magic, look at Lilac.

Archor tried to unravel the reels and only ended up with a big ball of coloured mess. After exerting his frustration, Archor realised his mother was not to blame, and he snipped the skin coloured gloves into pieces and vowel he would never allow anyone to humiliate him again. Archor had decided, if people would not be respectful of his feelings, then he would no longer let them in. Sure they could make fun of him, but they could not call themselves his friend. Archor decided he would close the door to his room and to his heart and would no longer visit Morden or Lilac, or the annual festival ever again.

The town of Tenderville and its Mayor had expanded over the years. The Mayor's eldest daughter was now fifteen, his son was thirteen and he had a nine year-old and twins that were six years old and yes, in her arms, his wife held a newborn.

"Hand the baby back, now Mildred," said the Mayor.

The baby was (of course) not hers. It belonged to someone else. But the Mayor's wife did love babies (an obvious statement to make when looking at her own brood).

The Mayor's wife passed the newborn baby back to its real mother and said, "Lovely dear, just lovely. Remember when ours were as small and precious as that, dear."

"Yes, dear," said the Mayor. He turned to his eldest daughter and said, "You were once that small," to

which the eldest daughter rolled her eyes and grunted. Harriet blew a bubble with her gum, popped it
with her heavily jewelled fingers and said, "Yeah,
sure dad."

"All baby's are adorable," said the Mayor's wife.

The Mayor agreed, and upon seeing the baby suck
its thumb he said to its mother, "Don't let the baby
suck its thumb, it'll end up with buck teeth and have
to go to rabbit school. Where it will learn how to nibble carrots, twitch its ears and dig holes. But at least
it will be able to find its way home in the dark."

The new mother looked the Mayor up and down,
scoffed and then turned and left in a huff.

"Don't upset the voters, dear," said his wife.

"Yes, dear," replied the Mayor.

Whilst the Mayor and his wife had been cooing over
another ladies new bundle of joy, he didn't notice one
of his twins was playing with the pair of scissors that
hung from the chain that was attached to his belt.
The six year old was fascinated with the sapphire in
the pivot of the scissors. The child opened and closed
the scissors continually. What the twin did not know
was, in Pakistan, a country a long, long, way a way,
some believed that scissors should never be idly
opened and closed without purpose — it causes bad
luck. But the six year old had never been to, or even
heard of the country Pakistan, nor of the myth, so

it was too late and the bad luck was released — and so was the elastic in the Mayors pants, because that had accidently been snipped too. Without warning, the Mayors pants fell down to his ankles. The Mayor giggled, embarrassed and said, "Look's like my diet must be working, Mildred."

"Or your elastic just broke, dear," replied his wife.

Neither knew this would be the beginning of their bad luck.

* * *

Archor stood in front of the orange juice stand owned by Mrs White. She was a short squat old lady with bad teeth and a crooked nose. She looked over the three bright orange dresses hanging off coat hangers that Archor held in his hand.

"Perfect. They are perfect. Thank you so much for dropping them off to us, Archor. We are so excited by our new orange uniforms, aren't we girls?"

"Yes Mum," replied Mrs White's daughters, Lilly and Rachel.

"Your mother is such a busy lady, so taking time to design and make us new uniforms is very much appreciated," said Mrs White.

Archor smiled and Mrs White looked him over, up and down, and then walked around him before saying, "My, you have grown into a handsome young man, Archor."

Archor squirmed and shifted his feet, "Thank you, Mrs White."

"Help yourself to some juice. My Lilly will pour you a cup. You remember my daughter Lilly?"

Archor smiled and nodded at Lilly, who seemed to be a younger replica of her mother.

"And Rachel?"

"Hello, Rachel," said Archor, who thought Rachel was an even closer replica of her mother than Lily.

"Lilly! Please serve Mr Chatelaine a big cup of juice."

"Oh, no thank you, Mrs White, Miss Lilly. I have to rush," said Archor, handing over the dresses. "Thank you, anyway. It was nice to see you all again, good-bye."

Archor made a speedy exit. He cut down between the lane of games and festival rides. It had been years since he had attended the annual orange and grape festival, and he felt now that he was almost seventeen, he had perhaps grown out of it. He had only come to deliver the dresses for his mother, but now that he was there, he seemed curious and interested to look around at the changes made, how things had grown, and pondered at the way things shifted and moved with time.

As he walked along the river bank, the paddle

boats all looked the same, only at the far end of the river was the tunnel-of-love's exit. The ride was now completed since Archor saw it last, and couples popped out of the end of the tunnel in their boats and floated out across the river. Some couples were still embraced and had no concern or care for on look-ers, others came out of the tunnel sitting as far apart from each other as possible. Some boys sheepishly wiped lip gloss from their lips and the girls giggled, some couples looked bored with the ride, and with each other.

"Have you been on the ride yet, Archor?"

Before Archor even turned to face the person who spoke, he knew instantly who it was. Lilac had grown tall and slender, her hair curled around her shoulders and her eyes no longer looked childish, but clear and thoughtful. And while she had changed in so many ways, she was still beautiful, perhaps more beautiful than before, more than Archor could even remember.

"This was where we stood the last time we were friends," said Lilac.

"Were still friends," said Archor, "I've just been busy."

"Do you still do magic, Archor?" asked Lilac.

"Just for myself, now, and sometimes for my mum."

"Do a trick for me, Archor. It's been years since I've seen a magic trick."

Archor pulled from his pocket a single playing card, it was the joker and as he shook it in his hand it magically turned into the queen of hearts.

"That was brilliant!" said Lilac.

"No, it's a trick Lilac, see there are two cards, one a joker and one a queen of hearts, I just flipped the card over. It's faster than your eye, so it looks like it magically transformed. Here you keep them, now that you know how it's done, you can practice."

Lilac took the cards and held them in her palm, she shook them, seeing if she could flick the cards over without Archor seeing, but instead she dropped both of them.

Archor picked up the fallen cards and handed them back, "Keep trying, Lilac. You'll get the hang of it."

Lilac hesitated, "So you still believe in magic?"

"No. I don't believe in it. All magic can be explained, Lilac. It's a trick, a puzzle, but it's not magic. If there was such thing as magic, then maybe I'm the magic that went wrong between my mother and my father. That magic disappeared between them, it disappeared from their marriage. Maybe that's why I wasn't born whole. The magic didn't work between them."

Lilac looked disappointed, "I thought I had shown you that you could believe, but you must have forgotten."

Archor felt ashamed, and was about to leave when Lilac stopped him and asked, "Can I see if there is just a little bit of magic left?"

"Pardon?"

"Let's go on all the rides, eat fairy floss, bob for apples, judge the apple pies, crush grapes, eat hot donuts rolled in sugar, and try the tunnel-of-love. Let's see if we can find the magic we once had."

Archor now felt the tunnel-of-love wasn't as dumb as he thought it was. What seemed stupid and ridiculous, now seemed like a nice place to be.

"Actually, I have to deliver some more garments for my mum, but would you like to meet up later? How about we meet at the tunnel-of-love at seven, we can both take our first ride together. Then have some dinner?"

"Okay, it's a date," Lilac stood up on her tippy toes and kissed Archor on the lips softly. She blushed and giggled, and in that moment she was just like the eleven year old Archor had always remembered.

Lilac skipped off and over her shoulder she called, "See you at seven o'clock, Archor. Don't be late."

*   *   *

While Archor was out running errands, Mrs Chatelaine was secretly working away at sewing Archor's seventeenth birthday present. She had finished making a jacket that she started to make a long, long time ago with glittery sequence cuffs. The inside was lined with black silk, and it had many hidden pockets for a magician to hide a rabbit, or a dove, or all the other wonderful things magicians used to create their illusions. The jacket had over sized long tails at the back and was perhaps one of the most fancy and smartest dinner jackets she had ever sewn.

The last time Mrs Chatelaine had sewn a magic costume was for her husband, many, many years ago, before Archor was even born. And back then she never had the chance to finish it. Now she was going to finish it and give it to Archor as a gift for his upcoming birthday.

But there were a few extra touches that Mrs Chatelaine had made to the original design of the jacket, which made it more fantastic, than just being a jacket. From all the off cut material customers had discarded and didn't want returned over the years, Mrs Chatelaine had kept them, collecting them, and she used these long slips of assorted coloured material to write in cross stitch all her hopes and dreams for Archor.

Over the last few months she had sat in the bay window under the old kerosene lamp, and late into the night with a needle and thread she sewed her words of hope, love, and good fortune. She sewed all the things a mother would ever wish for her son on these long strips of coloured material. So whilst Archor was running errands, Mrs Chatelaine went to work on her assortment of dreams and hopes.

*   *   *

Archor took a little too long in the shower, in fact, a person could have scrubbed themselves six times over in the time it took Archor to shower his body once.

Archor took a little too long in front of the mirror. A barber could have trimmed and styled four customers in the time it took Archor just to brush his hair.

Archor took forever to clean his teeth. A dentist could have pulled three teeth, completed one filling and had a coffee break in the time it took Archor to brush, floss, rinse, gargle and perfect his smile.

Archor took an eternity selecting his clothes. His mother could have sewn uniforms for a whole army in the time it took Archor to decide what to wear.

And Archor used way too much cologne, that all the dogs in the neighbourhood sneezed before he had even walked pass them.

On his way to the annual fete Archor stopped at

the florist and picked up a small bunch of daffodils so that by the time he arrived at the fair and made it to the tunnel-of-love it was already just after seven o'clock and Archor was too late.

Morden had beaten him to it.

Archor had arrived just in time to see Lilac and Morden hop into one of the boats and depart on the ride. The boat disappeared into the tunnel-of-love and Archor was sure he saw Morden take Lilac's hand. Not just take her hand, but make it very obvious that he had all five fingers and thumbs to hold her hand.

It couldn't be true? Archor couldn't believe what he had seen. Was he set up? Had they both done this on purpose? Archor raced along the riverbank towards the tunnels exit, and he made it just as Morden and Lilac's boat slid out of the tunnel and onto the river. Morden caught sight of Archor standing on the bank. He looked Archor in the eye, wiped his lips with his thumb and smiled at Archor. Then with all four fingers and his thumb he waved goodbye to Archor, and dropped the two playing cards into the water.

The two cards, the joker and the queen of hearts drifted apart, bobbing away from each other until they submerged under the water and sunk to the sludgy mud below.

If Archor had of been taught how to read his cards, instead of doing tricks with his cards, he would have known that the joker card was also the magician card, and that it points to the talents, resources and capabilities of the person, this is a message that they need to tap into their full potential rather than hold back, this card is about chance and transformation.

Archor had just had a chance meeting with Lilac, and over the years he had grown and transformed, he was almost at his destiny. But if Archor had of known what this card meant, instead of watching it float away and sink, he would have also known that this card meant there was a manipulator floating around (yes! in a tunnel-of-love boat!) and this other person did not have Archor's best interest in mind. But Archor never learnt to read the cards, or how to play cards, just how to do tricks with them.

As Archor stood on the bank, the queen of hearts, an image of beauty disappeared.

But Archor also noticed that from the back seat of Lilac's and Morden's floating boat a piece of paper flew out, and was picked up in the wind. It floated and zigzagged in the air, until it eventually landed at Archor's feet. It was a list of children's names, scrawled in thick carpenter's pencil, and all the things they wouldn't be able to do, if they didn't have their thumbs.

*   *   *

With the list of names scrunched in his fist, Archor saw the royal blue tapestry tent and its opening flap in the breeze far on the hill top. He gritted his teeth and marched up the hillside. Without invitation or warning, he thrust open the tent flap and stormed inside.

"I've been waiting for you, Archor."

All the bravado Archor had drained away at the sight of the mystic. She was more beautiful than Lilac. The mystic's eyes were hypnotic as a peacock's tail, her voice was delicate and enticing, it made Archor stand still, unable to move.

"Please, sit."

Archor could only manage to shake his head.

"It will be easier to hear, if you sit Archor. I know why you're here."

Archor swallowed.

"It's not your story that you have come to hear, but your fathers. Yes?"

Archor's eight fingers tingled. His lips formed the shape of the word 'yes' but he made no sound.

"It is the story that begins long before you were even born. A *long* story, so I suggest you sit."

Archor did not move.

The Mystic smiled, and began her story, "Your mother was very much in love with your father and your father loved her back just as much."

"Then why did he leave us?"

"He fell for the magical charm of another woman. He was foolish with his thoughts and emotions. Your mother was a performer herself. They were the great double act, he made rabbits and doves appear and disappear, but his greatest act was the appearance of your mother on stage. She would sew costumes that both delighted and shocked the audience. Her costumes magically changed a hundred times in every act. She would disappear and reappeared in something else, something more startling and yet delightfully more shocking than before. Your mother and father filled the theatre. It was not just your fathers great magic people came to see, men came to see your mother, her beauty, her presence, and the ladies came to see her clothes. The two were the most envied couple amongst the circus, the theatres and in society."

"Then what happened between them?"

"Your mother fell pregnant and with a baby on the way, the show had to go on. They were newly married, they had bills to pay, and those costumes were expensive. They sold some to the Lords and Ladies for their costume balls, some they sold to the movie houses, but they still owed, you see, there were hundreds of costumes, some never warn, because they didn't match your mother's beauty."

The mystic paused and sipped her green tea, "Please Archor, sit and have some tea."

"No."

"May I read your list?"

"After you have finished the story."

"Very well," the Mystic le Fay continued, "your father hired someone else to help him with his act. She had to also understand magic, be beautiful, and ..."

"He fell in love with her? Whilst my mother was pregnant with me, he just fell for another woman."

"Not just any old woman, Archor. Your mother was in the middle of making your father a new costume, and when she went to try it on him, she found them on stage, together in an embrace, and you see she had scissors in her hand."

"It was you! And she stabbed my father?"

"Yes! No! Archor!"

Archor dropped the list and fled.

*　　*　　*

Mrs Chatelaine was thrilled that Archor had left for the evening to have dinner and see the fete with Lilac. Thrilled in so many ways. She decided that after hearing this great news, this great turn of events for her son, it was the perfect time to pin all her hopes for him onto his jacket.

As Mrs Chatelaine picked up the cotton reel and started to unwind some thread she came to the end of the cotton. She grabbed another cotton reel and it too was out of thread. It was the first time that Mrs Chatelaine had ever run out of thread. She pulled the cotton from reel to reel, and was left with wooden bobbins. She searched the house, but could not find a single reel with a decent thread of cotton for sewing. She felt as unravelled as the reels. Mrs Chatelaine had run out of thread and had nothing left to pin her son's hopes on.

✻   ✻   ✻

Archor crept back into the house late at night. He did not want to come home when his mother was still up, otherwise she would want to hear all about it and Archor had nothing to say.

On the coffee table was his father's old wand. Archor dropped it to the floor and stomped on it. When he removed his foot, the wood had split and pointed like an arrow.

"West," whispered Archor. "I'll head west, way beyond the orange trees. Beyond the grape vines."

Archor looked in the direction the arrow pointed and in the small dining room his eye caught sight of the jacket Mrs Chatelaine had left hanging over the backrest of one of the chairs.

It was exquisite.

Archor tried it on and it was a perfect fit, then he picked up his mothers shearing scissors and left the house. It would be many years before Archor would return and his mother would be able to show him all the hopes she had for him.

Hopes stitched on strips of coloured fabric.

Life without two thumbs
The Sonnet of the Thumb Thief

Snip, snap, ends that, your life without two thumbs.
O don't be sad, livid and mad inside —
deride — your hands are mine. O be benumb!
It's how I must condemn someone for chide.
Play your silent notes. Snip! You're wilt of song.
Snap! Wilt of hope. I've sponged your ambitions
and grief's ahead. The cost of dreams are gone
with the swoop of my wand. Vile magician.
Do you think I ache? Ha! You think I quake?
Show sorrow or grieve a life that's unfair?
No! I just take what's mine, thumbs. You'll awake
and the sunrise will reveal your nightmare.
    But there's still hope, a chance on your chaste part,
    because I left you with your eyes and heart.

Archor left Tenderville whistling the sonnet of the thumb thief. Behind him he pulled a wagon stolen from the orange orchards. Marmalade jars clanked and chinked and rattled in the back of the wagon. Only these jars were not filled with the sweet taste of breakfast marmalade, these jars were filled with something far more sinister, far more vile and grisly. Yes, inside these jars floated things that were very macabre indeed.

Fourteen years later

Fourteen years had passed since Archor Chatelaine had left the town of Tenderville. Fourteen times the cherry blossom trees had budded pink flowers; fourteen harvests of oranges had been picked, packed and delivered across the country; fourteen times the grapes had been picked and crushed and bottled into wine; fourteen times since Archor had left town, Lilac had visited the river where the tunnel-of-love once gave couples a ride that would change their relationship, forever.

A lot had happened in fourteen years. Morden was now thirty-one years old and married to Lilac. They were also the proud parents of a ten-year-old son, named Garnet.

Lilac and Morden lived in a chocolate coloured house with blue windows. Their son, Garnet, had the best room in the house. A room with an enormous window that looked over the whole of Main Street. Garnet could see his friends coming to visit for miles. He could watch all of Tenderville go about their business in a way that Garnet had only known them too, because Garnet had never seen what Tenderville was like *before* they had their thumbs cut off.

Yes, the town of Tenderville had changed.

You see, without thumbs, people could not turn keys, so they couldn't lock their doors. If you can't lock your valuable things away, then you must learn to trust each other, respect each other's belongings and be honest.

Without their thumbs, girls couldn't sew nice clothes, or plait their hair, or paint their nails or put on their make-up, so people had to be careful of others feelings, careful of their words and not comment or judge how others looked. Everyone had to be respectful, kind, and never say bad things about what others wore, or what their hair looked like. Everyone was nice, very nice, very nice and respectful, and courteous. Girls wore hand-me-downs, or dresses they made themselves. But instead of poking fun at what they wore, thumbless people knew they had to be kind, tactful.

"Nice dress Mary-Lou," called the thumbless postie as he rode past on his push bike.

"Thank you, Mr Peterson! Happy deliveries!" replied the thumbless Mary-Lou.

"Thank you, Mary-Lou."

"You're welcome, Mr Peterson."

And because Mr Peterson had no thumbs to ring the bell on his bike when over taking pedestrians on the footpath, he had to politely ask them to move. After fourteen years of asking people to 'mind behind them, the Postie is coming through,' everyone in Tenderville knew his voice, knew him, and said hello, good morning, and have a nice day. Mr Peterson enjoyed his job of delivering the mail of Tenderville, but he loved it all the more since he lost his thumbs.

See, everyone in Tenderville was nice, very nice, very *boring-ly* nice ...

Without thumbs, people could not paint their homes very well, shop signs were a little wobbly, and plant hedges were trimmed and cut askew. The town was not perfect to look at. It was *un*-perfect in so many ways; it looked a little asymmetrical, skee-wiff, lop-sided, messy. But nobody took any notice, because everyone had learnt to never judge or say a negative remark, because that was the way life was without thumbs.

Without thumbs, Tenderville was the most tender place to live on earth. Everything worked out perfectly for all those who had lost their thumbs all those long, long years ago. But for those with thumbs, they saw things a little differently.

Mrs Chatelaine and Lilac were the only two people that Archor had left with their thumbs still attached. But Mrs Chatelaine was now aging, and her hands and her thumbs could not keep up with the demand for pretty dresses.

Because Lilac had thumbs she would be stopped in the street and asked by kids to do things that required thumbs. She plaited girl's hair, sewed on teddy bear eyes that had fallen off. She was always pleased to do this, but inside she felt guilty that she was left with her thumbs and forever reminded of Archor.

Mrs Chatelaine opened jars, turned off taps, and removed button's and bows, and sewed *Velcro* strips to all the garments and shoes and bags, and anything that you needed two thumbs to open. More importantly, when ever there was a wedding Mrs Chatelaine was asked to make the dress, and Lilac to do the brides hair and make-up. Mrs Chatelaine also trimmed the groom's fringe to make sure it was straight and even, and pluck the ear hairs of the bride's father. Weddings with all their bows, and pretty bits became very exhausting for both Lilac and Mrs Chatelaine, the only two people capable of making things look perfect.

Mrs Chatelaine hated her thumbs, and Lilac felt

guilty for hers. They did not feel the tenderness of Tenderville at all.

Archor had no idea, that the two people he loved the most, were Tenderville's most miserable.

＊　　＊　　＊

There were some other changes in Tenderville. The thing was, all the people who had lost their thumbs fourteen years ago, had now grown up. They were all thumbless adults and had children of their own, children born *with* thumbs. The thumbless adults were so frightened that the Thumb Thief would return and take the thumbs of their children, that Tenderville put in place a Law that stated all thumbs were to be covered and not used in public.

That's right. The children of the thumbless parents had to cover their thumbs. The Mayor of Tenderville (who knew how expensive it was to raise children, having had five of his own) came up with a genius idea, that would cost the town nothing. Yes, the Mayor had an idea for free thumb covers. All children under five wore a grape on their thumb, and anyone over five had an orange on their thumb. This was the cheapest and most economical option and all parents were supplied the fruit for free (to the cost of the local council, of course). Oh, they had tried many other contraptions before they had discovered this solution. There was;

- the cage
- the hidden mirror trick that made it look like a thumb was not there
- the sticky wrap that wrapped the thumb against the pointer finger, so it looked like one big fat finger
- The thumbless glove, where the thumb and pointer finger shared the same slot
- and many other disastrous and medieval contraptions that were hideous, uncomfortable and unpractical

At last the Mayor decided that the grapes and oranges the town grew could also protect their children. So not only did Tenderville supply oranges and grapes, orange and grape juice and orange and grape jam (which is also call marmalade or English breakfast), it also supplied thumb protectors.

The thumbless adults felt proud of their town, their ideas, and their way of life. But the next generation, the thumbed generation started to feel cheated and angry because they were not allowed to play music, they were never taught how to play a musical instrument, they never played sport, never knew how to sew, how to plait hair, paint nails, sketch, cook, decorate a cake, and only saw their thumbs at night when they bathed.

*　　*　　*

The town's Mayor no longer sported fancy scissors. There was no ribbon to cut and no fate to attend. That had closed down fourteen years ago. Instead, in the town centre the Mayor would stand on the sandstone edge of the town's water fountain and read out aloud a Homily, a kind of long boring sermon that told the town (over and over again, year after year — for fourteen years to be exact) that it's very wrong to cut off people's thumbs.

But upon listening to *'Protecting the thumbs of children'* or as the Mayor liked to title it, *'A homily against the disobedience and wilful rebellion by cutting off others thumbs'* it seemed somewhat pointless to everyone in Tenderville, and nobody paid attention to it. The Homily was only aimed at the one boy who cut their thumbs off, and he had left town a long, long time ago.

The Mayor was also tired of this speech, but regardless, he still prattled on. Little did he know some people secretly wished that the boy called Archor had cut off their tongues, instead of their thumbs, and they would not have to listen to the speech the Mayor recited every year.

The orange and grape festival was no longer about celebration, it was about protection. Protection of thumbs and a dull speech. The town had lost its fun when they lost their thumbs.

The Mayor was almost sixty and a grandfather and was soon to retire. This should have made him happy, but something felt like it was missing, and it wasn't just his thumbs. He would let his grandchildren climb all over him. When one started to insert a finger up his nose the Mayor laughed and said, "Do you know if you stick your finger up a person's nose–" But his wife and eldest daughter gasped, and quickly hush him, "Shh!"

The Mayor looked at his grandchildren's thumbs in oranges and grapes and closed his mouth and looked sullen. His grandchildren may have had their thumbs, but they weren't having any fun.

"Okay, kids," said the Mayor, "Off you get, I have to read the Homily to the town of Tenderville."

"Why? It's boring."

"One day you will understand."

The grandchildren all groaned and the Mayor missed the good old days when he used to open the season with the cutting of the ribbon and the opening of the fair. But now the rides and attractions had been closed down and taped off. They were old and crumbling. Since everyone became thumbless, the attractions and rides no longer operated. The old fairground looked like a ghost town.

* * *

The old Mayor was not the only one who wished the fair was still operating, Morden's son, Garnet, noticed the F on the sign *Fun-Parlour* had fallen off, leaving just the word *un*. It was an *un-Parlour*. And it was exactly how Garnet felt about the town, un-bearable, un-appealing, un-done and un-lucky to live in Tenderville.

Listening to a Homily wasn't a fun day, it was an un-day. Garnet wished he could see what the town use to be like when everything was in operation. The way it was when his dad was a boy. And Garnet had made this almost possible.

Almost.

Garnet and his friends would sneak away and head down towards the old fair ground. They would climb under the faded safety tape and have the whole fate to themselves. While it had not operated for four-teen years, the boys could still smell caramel in the air, almost hear the sound of the merry-go-round, the voices of the crowd, and feel a certain energy in the air. It gave them all goose bumps, a tingly feeling, a creepy feeling like they had stepped back in time.

Inside the big top the boys took off their oranges. Garnet and his friends played music with the old abandoned instruments and because they were never taught how to play, they blew and banged brass, and made it all up. They skipped rope, played handball, some of the boys even wrote poetry across the side wall of the tent, others painted murals. They all sang songs, tried to strum guitars, play flutes from the wrong end, conducted imaginary orchestras and pretended the sound they made was a brilliant masterpiece. The point was, they were having fun with their thumbs.

Some of the boys recited *Hamlet* and *Romeo and Juliet* and did such a bad job of it that they giggled and laughed so hard that they all agreed they would apologise to Shakespeare himself. If they had of known *Othello* they would have recited that too, but Garnet had not read or learnt that one yet. They turned on the stage lights, and perform shadow puppets against the stage backdrop. They put on an impromptu show and did all the wonderful, joyful, delightful things you can do when you have your thumbs.

But on this day, the wind was not their friend. On this particular day, the wind carried the sound into town and the Mayor, his wife, Harriet and her children, the postman, Mary-Lou, Susan, Rose, Debbie,

Dean, Alex, Greg, Carlos, Mr Hollingsworth, Morden and Lilac, and all the other parents heard the music — and were horrified. The Mayor turned towards the place where the big top once stood tall and inviting, and his face flushed pale. The parents all looked in the same direction. No one needed to speak, for they all knew the sound was made with the use of thumbs. Un-protected thumbs. The crowd raced down the cobbled street towards the sound as fast as they could.

They snapped the safety tape and raced towards the entrance of the old red and white striped tent. It leaned to the side and the roof had sunken in, but the sound that flowed out the doors was strictly forbidden. The Mayor was the first to step inside. The music and lights were so bright it shocked them all.

"STOP!"

Under the old big top Morden and Lilac quivered. On stage it was their son in the centre with his thumbs exposed.

"How could you possibly be involved in this, Garnet?" Morden was outraged.

"We were just–"

"How could you?"

"We just wanted to play, with our thumbs," pleaded Garnet.

"Put your thumbs back on, it's for your protection."

"I can't, I ate them."

"You ate your thumbs?"

"No dad, yes, I ate my oranges. I was hungry."

"Cover them up, Garnet. Cover your thumbs."

"No."

"It's the Law, Garnet. Now cover your thumbs."

"No, dad. I'm not covering them up anymore. I want to have fun. Back in your time you had fun."

"That's because we had thumbs." Morden pleaded, "Please Garnet, you have to keep your oranges on your thumbs!" Morden mounted up onto the stage. He lashed out and tried to grab Garnet's wrist, but Garnet yanked his arm away, tripping and falling backwards off the stage.

"Garnet!"

On the ground Garnet lay in a haze, his face looked scorned with ill thoughts. He scrambled to his feet and fled the circus tent.

"Garnet! Wait!" Morden tried to call his sons name again, but he had lost his voice. The air had left his throat, and he was soundless. Morden felt a sob of empathy in the back of his throat. His throat constricted and tightened. He clenched his teeth and squeezed his jaw shut to hold back the sobs in his chest. His mind was flooded with the memory of a magic show. He felt the pain of recalling the evening when the audience had laughed at the thumbless boy on stage, and now here Morden was, many years later, standing on that very same stage, thumbless himself.

⁂   *   *

Garnet ran as fast as he could from his father and the old circus tent. But he had never ventured further than the orange orchards, never seen what was beyond them, so he had no idea where he could run and hide. On a far away hill top, he saw a royal blue tent of faded tapestry prints flap in the breeze. It was a perfect place to hide. Garnet scrambled up the hill with his fists clenched tight. He slipped in through the tents opening and expected it to be dark inside. Instead, it was lit with coloured candles in clear glass tubes that hung from brass chains from the pitch in the roof. Some candles were behind patterned stain-glass domes. On the floor hundreds of coloured cushions scattered the ground. There was a smell of spice and a sweet floral scent, a mix that he could not remember where he had smelt it before, but it felt familiar to him. It was the most beautiful room he had ever seen.

"Hello, Garnet."

Garnet yelped and stepped back. Amongst the colour he had not seen the woman behind the table.

She was colourful and as vivid as the room. Captivating with her strange eyes of turquoise and gold.

"Don't be afraid."

"I'm not," said Garnet.

"Are you here for a story?"

"Ha?"

"That's what I do, tell stories."

"I thought you would tell peoples fortunes," said Garnet.

"It's the same thing. It's the story of their life. I am The Mystic le Fay. Please sit and I'll tell you a story."

"What type of story?"

"Let me tell you a story about a pair of scissors," said the Mystic le Fay.

Garnet swallowed trying to show that he was not scared by a silly story about scissors.

"Did you know in some parts of North Africa, it is believed that scissors can be a curse to a groom and his bride?"

"No?" said Garnet. Somehow Garnet felt he didn't really want to hear the end of this story. He flinched when the mystic smiled, but her voice lulled him deep into her story. So deep that he forgot why he had entered the tent in the first place.

"Once there was a young man who fell deeply in love with a lady. He was not from her society, not welcomed in her family and sneered at by her friends. But the lady thought he was the most exotic and magical person she had ever met. She would tell her mother and friends she was off to see the opera, when really she went down town to the small wooden theatre to see the hansom magician perform his tricks.

"In the old dusty theatre she would nibble Gaz, a honey and pistachio flavoured nougat that the young man brought for her each night in a white box with a red bow. After the show they would get ice-cream together that was flavoured with saffron and rose water. As they walked under the canopy of the pink blossom trees, she would try and guess how he did his tricks, and he would be impressed at her cleverness.

"She was warned by her father to, 'stay away from that filthy scoundrel, he'll only bring you no good', but she did not listen. The two would meet after the show, share a bowl of pasta and all their secrets of the things that would make them happy in life, and it turned out, they had the same secrets.

"So, one night, she packed her bag and waited for him to collect her. He showed up on the back of a fantastic white stallion, borrowed from the circus where he had just been employed. The horse neighed, stood up on its hind legs, and the hansom magician reached out his hand and helped her up onto the back of the horse. She sat behind him and wrapped her arms around his waist. And they galloped off to a new life together.

"But, when the groom was with his bride-to-be on horseback, they had no idea her father was standing at the bedroom window with a pair of scissors in his hand. You see, the myth is, the person who is enacting the curse would stand behind the groom and call out his name. If the groom answered to his name being called, the scissors would then be snapped shut and the groom would have an unhappy marriage with his bride, and the couple would be cursed forever. And that is exactly what happened to this couple. He answered to his name being called, and at that precise moment, her father snapped the scissors shut."

"That's a stupid story," said Garnet. He wanted to leave. He didn't want to hear any more. "Nothing really happened to them, they both got away."

"I'm not finished yet. They were cursed. Together they ran off to join the circus and became the most famous double act there ever was. They were married, wealthy and soon to have their first child."

"That doesn't sound like a curse to me."

"The show had to go on, but the baby was growing fast and the costumes that people came to see his wife wear no longer fitted, so they had to find another young and beautiful lady who would fit the costumes and keep the show going. But the husband began to lust after this other woman. He was captivated by her beauty. He lost his mind and his morals. One night after a performance when all the theatre seats were empty and they were the only two left on stage, they embraced and kissed."

Garnet winced, dropped his eyes and felt sorry for the wife, "Your story is sad, but I can't see the curse. I just see a foolish man who was immoral."

"Don't rush a good story, boy. I'm getting there."

"Just when they locked lips on stage, the husband's wife entered. She was the one who sewed all their garments and was a brilliant designer of theatrical costumes. She pushed through the theatre doors, her large round stomach with her first child filled the isle, and in her hand she held a new jacket for her husband and a pair of scissors in her other hand. She needed to make the final adjustments, she just wanted him to try it on one last time, but instead she found them together, lips locked. She turned and ran back up the aisle."

Garnet cocked an eyebrow, "Poor husband, and poor timing, I still can't see the curse."

The Mystic smiled, "As she raced up the isle she tripped, you know, you should never run with scissors in your hand. And she fell on the scissor blades which sliced cleanly into her stomach and snipped off the thumbs off her unborn child."

Garnet paled.

"There is your curse. Happy now, boy?"

"That's a terrible story."

"I've never heard of a nice curse."

"I need to go," said Garnet.

"Not yet, boy. This story is not finished. You see, words are powerful shackles, and Sir, you look like you are the key to unlocking those shackles. The Thumb Thief had no thumbs, but chose to do things a different way. Your father has no thumbs and has chosen not to do things at all, and you have thumbs, and have chosen not to use them, except in secret. I think if you expose all secrets, everyone will learn to accept and live with or without their thumbs. They will learn to live in harmony and not fear."

"You want me to find every ones thumbs?"

The mystic smiled, "Yes, Garnet. You are the closest person to the key."

*   *   *

Garnet never returned home that evening. Instead he had run away to hunt for the thumbs of Tenderville. Garnet thought if he could return the missing thumbs of the thumbless, then everyone would be the same again and Tenderville could return to the way it was when his father was a boy.

Garnet travelled for five days.

On the first day he sat on the back of a penny-fathering pushbike. Its owner stood and rode, while Garnets bones rattled over every stone and pebble. The bike had an enormous wheel at the front and a small wheel at the back, and only one hard seat. Garnet was grateful for the ride, all the same.

On the second day Garnet travelled by a pump trolley. He met a man along the railroad who called out, 'If you get on the other end of my Kalamazoo, we will be able to hand pump this carriage twice as fast along the railway line.' Garnet was grateful, but his arms were tied by the end of the day.

On the third day Garnet met a Gypsy who said, 'You're welcome to sit on my donkey, but not in my caravan.' The donkey tried to nip his ankles, and smelt of hay and dung, but Garnet was grateful all the same.

On the fourth day, Garnet travelled downstream on a paddle wheeler, he was given free passage in return for scrubbing the deck and polishing the brass balls and handrails. Garnet's hands blistered, but he was grateful all the same.

On the fifth day Garnet travelled by foot. He smelt the air, saw bugs and birds, and felt the sun on his face, he listened to the wind through the tall trees, noticed the colour of the fields, the height of the surrounding mountains, and the shades of clouds. He saw what the world looked like outside of Tenderville — and it was big.

6. Garnet had travelled for five days to see for himself the *Great Fantastique Merveilleux Magician Extraordinaire*. Why? Because he was told that this magician performed the best tricks the world had ever seen — all with only eight fingers, and no thumbs.

*   *   *

Garnet arrived at the end of a lush green field where the beech trees began to grow. From the limbs of the beech trees white-paper Chinese lanterns hung. Garnet had never seen such beauty. Deeper into the woods large oak trees hung crystal chandeliers, each filled with a hundred lit candles. Ladies and Gentlemen sipped sparkling champagne from long crystal flutes. The women either wore white feather boas or long white fur coats, and the men wore white cravats and white leather shoes. The carpet leading into the enormous silver tent was not red, but white, and the children ate white floss on silver sticks, not pink.

Garnet was not wearing white, and his presence

was obvious. He stood behind the trunk of a large oak tree and waited for the guests to enter and then he quietly slipped through the side flaps.

Inside the circus tent, Garnet heard the orchestra before he saw the pit in which they sat. All their instruments were either white or silver and in the centre was an opera singer. Her voice was incredible and she sung notes that Garnet had never heard or knew were possible. Her face was powdered with white pancake make-up and her lips plum and in the shape of a love heart. Around her white doves and butterflies fluttered and flapped, landing on the tips of the bows of violins or rested on the corners of music stands.

Garnet sat alone through the entire show and saw stilt walkers, clowns, ballerinas, a white tiger and his tamer, a strong man, a whip cracker, dare devil, dancing white ponies and a trampoline act, what he did not see was;

1. a ballerina in silvery white tights with a ladder in them
2. a clown that hid a ticket stub in his belt for the midnight movie screening next door
3. a stilt walker that carried a photograph of his great grandfather during the war
4. a trampoline artist who wore her mother's locket
5. the lion tamer's lucky rabbit foot

6. the strong man's broken watch
7. a clown's hairpin that had a real diamond in it
8. the whip cracker who had smeared lipstick on his cheek
9. the dare devil that never took off her helmet and smelt of lavender
10. the bearded lady with the bald spot
11. and one of the clowns had wet paint under his shoes

At last, what everyone had been waiting for, the *Great Fantastique Merveilleux Magician Extraordinaire* appeared on stage with his dazzling assistant. The audience was captivated by the thumbless magician with eight fingers, and his thumbed assistant with ten fingers.

It was no hallucination, the audience was enchanted by the assistants extra digits and the magicians missing digits. Together on stage they were more than an extravaganza, they were a wonderland, a dream world, and ingenious duo of fantastical visions.

The opera singer ended her dolce note, and the musicians hushed their instruments. The Great Fantastique Merveilleux smiled at the audience, opened his arms and said, "Each of us has dark and light in us. It is up to you if you want to see the dark or the light. And you can change what you see by simply blinking. I ask you, if you please, blink!"

Garnet and the audience blinked and the Great Fantastique Merveilleux's costume turned black. His assistant's white glittering dress also turned black with the pattern of a spider's web around her neck. The audience gasped, and the Great Fantastique Merveilleux laughed and said, "Oh please, I am not that murky, am I? Blink again!"

Garnet and the audience blinked, and this time the pair up on stage wore rose pink costumes with flamingo feathers, and the audience erupted in applause.

Garnet had seen enough, and did not stay for the end of the show. Instead he made a quick exit out of the circus tent.

While the eight and ten finger couple astonished the audience with illusions, Garnet hunted for the thumbs of Tenderville. He searched the caravans, inside all the tents, every animal cage, every trunk, every costume van, every game stand and every prize display. He shuttered at the thought, but he still double checked the sausage stand (just in case). Garnet searched the private vans of the circus performers that were oddly more interesting than the rides and games, until he came to the last circus trailer. Unlike the others, this trailer had no garish images or murals painted on the side. It was not bright or brash like the other trailers. It was dull, rusted and coated in cobwebs. This trailer looked untouched, neglected, and like it held a haunted secret behind its doors. Garnet climbed up the metal ladder and slipped inside. The trailer had a pungent smell, almost a suffocating odour. He flicked on the light switch and it instantly illuminated hundreds of marmalade jars on shelves, the jars were stacked to the roof. Inside the jars were thumbs. Thumbs of different colours and sizes were floating on the bottom of each jars, they were not in shackles like the Mystic had described.

Garnet was confused, because they were not locked away, instead, they looked like pickled thumbs. Each jar was labelled with a name and on one of those jars was a label with *Morden's Thumbs.* Garnet had found his father's thumbs. With trembling hands, just as he reached up and took the jar with his father's name on it, four fingers snatched his wrist and Garnet dropped the jar.

The Ringmaster laughed at the frightened boy, but the magician with eight fingers did not laugh at all.

"Who are you?"

"Garnet, my name is Garnet."

"Garnet with fresh thumbs. Looks like they have never been used. Where are you from, Garnet?"

"Tenderville."

"Get out. *Get out!*" cried the eight fingered magician.

The Ringmaster hushed and put his hand gently on the magicians back and said to Garnet, "Many, many years ago, I performed in the town of Tenderville and called a small boy onto the stage with me to perform a trick, only half way through my performance I thought I had accidently removed the boy's thumbs by magic. It was not magic, it was a mistake. What wasn't a mistake was fourteen years later, that same boy came to me asking for a job, and turned my failing circus into the grandest and greatest show there could ever be. So when someone upsets my star attraction, I want to know why?"

Garnet swallowed, "I've come to collect the thumbs that belong to the people of Tenderville."

"Who asked you to do this?"

"The Mystic le Fay," said Garnet.

The magician frowned. "She is the cause of all this. She practices the art of deceit, not magic. She stole the heart of my father from my mother. Because of her deception, I have never met my father."

Garnet was not sure where he had plucked his courage from, but he was bold enough to answer, "No, that's not all together true. Your father could never forgive himself for you losing your thumbs, so he left because he felt ashamed. He could not live with the disappointment of his son knowing he was responsible for the loss of his thumbs."

The magician laughed, "Rubbish. Anyone from Tenderville does not deserve their thumbs. Stick out your thumb so it's easier for me to snip."

Garnet flinched, but the magician gripped his wrist tight, and from his silk pocket he took out a silver pair of shearing scissors with long sharp blades. The magician looked deep into Garnets eyes and saw a fleck of violet. The magician blinked and looked again.

Sometimes even though a thing isn't even yours, you love it so much, that even *you* want to protect it. The magician knew in a micro-second he could never, ever, harm a child of Lilac.

"Wait!" Morden burst through the trailer door. The sound of Morden's voice made the magician clench the young boy's wrist tighter.

Morden pleaded, "Please, take my fingers, take my toes, but spare my son's thumbs."

"Your son?" The magician and Morden faced each other, and then the magician hissed to Garnet, "Your father is also thief. He stole my true love from me. Now who do you think is the villain?"

"Perhaps I did Archor, and I know it's hard to believe, but I always loved Lilac as much as you did."

Archor gulped at the sound of his name. He had not heard it spoken aloud for more than fourteen years. He snarled, "By missing my thumbs I missed the fifth thing in life, friendship. Yes, tell your son all about our friendship, Morden."

Garnet swallowed and tried to squirm his wrist out of Archor's grip, "You know, Archor, friendship can't be counted on fingers, but only in your heart."

Archor gripped Garnets arm tighter and hissed, "But I cut that off, see young boy, I took all of Tenderville's friendships and made them all enemies."

"No, you didn't. By taking away every ones thumbs, it only opened the heart of Tenderville even more. It bought everyone together, it did not break them apart." And then Garnet remembered what the Mystic had said, 'What if you could change a person's life, by changing the words you spoke to them?' and Garnet pleaded, "Archor, please come back to Tenderville? There are some people who miss you dearly and want to see you."And in that one small moment, those gentle spoken words were like a key that unlocked the shackles of the Scissor Man. His face began to soften. Not for a long time had he felt his heart pound in his chest. A lightness over came him.

He slowly let go of Garnets arm, and ten loving fingers touched his shoulders and said, "Archor, I think it's time to go home and introduce your wife to your mother, and to your friend, Lilac."

*   *   *

When Archor first arrived at the circus, he was in need of a friend and the Ringmaster was in need of a miracle. Archor was the Ringmaster's miracle, and Lucidity became Archor's friend first, and then his wife.

It was a beautiful wedding inside the big top, with all the performers and animals as witnesses. The Ringmaster closed the show for a whole day and night so that all the circus performers could celebrate, eat, drink and be merry. They each performed tricks, juggled with fire, and filled the tent with glitter. It was one of the most spectacular shows ever, and it was all just for the performers, the family who all lived under the big top.

Three days before the wedding, Archor proposed to Lucidity while they played and swung on the high trapeze. Something that they did for fun. But before Archor gave Lucidity the ring (which had taken months for him to save up and pay for), he first told her his story. His whole story. His truthful story, even though it was an ugly story.

Lucidity listened to this story, and then she told a story of her own. A tall story ...

A Tall Story,
by Miss Lucidity Polydactalovely

Once upon a time, there was a village tucked away behind mint coloured mountains. It was kept warm under a toffee coloured sun and built on slate, sandstone and harmony. On the west side of the village there lived a young man, and in the east there lived a young lady. When they stood together, they made a couple.

On the day of their wedding, the priest turned to the guests and said, "Should anything be broken in this couple's marriage, then let it be this glass." The priest placed a glass wrapped in white linen before the grooms' feet. When the groom stomped on the glass, it did not break. Sheepish, the groom tried again, but still the glass would not break.

The priest didn't want the groom to look foolish in front of the bride-to-be, so he stomped on the glass. As if to defy the work of God, the glass did not break.

The priest turned to the guests and said, "If anyone thinks they can ensure that the only thing in this marriage to break will be this glass, please feel free to come up to the front of the church, and stomp on it."

The bride's father was first, but the glass did not break. The groom's father and all three brothers tried, still, the glass kept its perfect form. The best man, the bridesmaids and groomsmen, the guests and even the blind organ player tried and the glass remained intact — it did not break.

The wedding ceremony couldn't continue. It was a catastrophe. The priest cleared his throat and said, "Perhaps we could fill this glass with milk, and meet again next week, for if anything is to go sour in this relation-ship, then let it be this glass of milk."

The guests agreed. The unbreakable glass was filled with milk, placed on the altar and the congregation went home.

A week later, the guests returned for the wedding. Sadly, it was in vain, for the milk had not soured.

"Cheese!" said a guest. "I will bring a lump of my goat's cheese to the altar. And if anything is to go mouldy in this marriage, let it be my goat's cheese."

The guest all agreed.

Yet another week later, they returned. The milk and lump of cheese was perfect.

The woodchopper cried, "Wood! If anything is to rot in this marriage, let it be a piece of wood."

The florist suggested, "Flowers! If anything is to wilt in this couples relationship, let it be the bride's bouquet."

Each week a guest would bring something.

"If anything is to collapse, then let it be this house of cards."

"If anything is to go bad, then let it be the eggs from my hen."

"If anything is to spoil, then let it be my homemade chutney, pickles and jams."

"If anything is to breakdown, wear and tear, or rust-" But the guests drew the line at Percy wanting to park his automobile at the altar.

The weeks turned into months. The months turned into years. Nothing wilted, rotted, bent, smelt, soured, decayed, crumbled, eroded, decomposed, deteriorated, expired, shrivelled or perished. Every item brought to the altar remained in perfect form.

Many seasons, sunrises, and moon cycles passed. Together the couple were almost a century times two, and still not married. Both waiting for something other than their marriage to ruin, fall apart, break, rot, crumble … anything!

On the bride-to-be's one hundredth birthday, she said to her aged fiancé, "Perhaps nothing will ever go wrong with our marriage, and it will be perfect."

"You are right," said the groom. "Tomorrow, let's get married."

The very next morning the old couple were wed. The day was perfect in every way and so was the couple's marriage. They never fought, never argued, and only said the nicest, kindest, loving things to each other. Theirs was a perfect marriage indeed.

The day after their wedding, they both died.

When Lucidity finished her story, Archor knew that this was the woman he wanted to spend the rest of his life with. Three days later they were wed under the big top, and there was no breaking of glass, no milk, and the only wood, was the wood they sat on, and the cheese they ate, and the flowers were beautiful, and that is all there is to say.

The winds of change
or
A short apology for Archor Chatelaine

Things change. Things always change.

Archor returned to Tenderville in his caravan of thumbs. He asked the town for their forgiveness and handed each person back their thumbs, perfectly preserved in their marmalade jars. And while this seems a simple thing to do, never underestimate how hard it is to admit your actions are wrong — or how hard it is to give forgiveness.

But time heals and the town of Tenderville went on.

Mr Hollingsworth had retired, but before receiving his gold watch, he re-painted the sign for the fair and took extra care painting the F back in the word Fun. It was now, once again a fun fair, not an un-fair.

Tenderville also realised they didn't need all those fancy rides and returned to the traditional fair of cattle judging, jam and pickled fruit competitions, orange tossing, bobbing for grapes, pie tossing, milking cows in record times, sheep shearing, flower and cake decorating, the school band played music and there was a talent show for the locals with a few budding magicians.

But while things returned to the ways of old, there are some things (just like a Christmas tree), that you just can't let go of, and in the town of Tenderville, living up to its name, they had to keep the tunnel-of-love. Too many people had fond memories of this very special ride.

The town's Mayor had also retired and had more grandchildren than he could ever wish for. The grandkids adored the old Mayor and they climbed all over him and pulled at his gray whiskers until he'd yelp and his daughter would yell at her children and say, "Don't yank the whiskers on your granddaddies chin or you'll make his toes curl up."

And when her youngest daughter poked out her tongue, her mother (the Mayor's eldest daughter, now grown with a brood of children of her own) repeated the wisdom of her father, "Keep your tongue in your mouth Harriet Junior, or a crow will think it's a worm and swoop down and pluck it from your mouth."

Her daughter instantly shut her mouth, and then her mother added, "When I was your age I never behaved like that!"

This statement only made the Mayor and his daughter roar with laughter and the grandkids think them odd. The old Mayor of Tenderville couldn't have been happier with the life he had provided, or of the town he lived in, or of his children and wife. His grandkids pinched coins from his wallet that hung from a chain, and the whole time he pretended he didn't notice.

*   *   *

Garnet and his friends were so unbelievably delighted by the immense feeling of freedom to be able to use their thumbs, they flew kites, drew along the footpaths in chalk, climbed trees, played ball, built billy-carts, picked flowers, made hand puppets, did cartwheels, played instruments, played clapping games, skipped rope; they did all the things they had only ever hoped they could try. They had a go at everything and helped everyone try something they had never done before. It was a time of great joy for them all.

*   *   *

Morden, Lilac and Archor were friends again. And they adored Archor's wife, Lucidity, and even more, they loved her ten fingered hands that seemed to always beat them in a game of cards, or to the last piece of pie, or were wrapped around Archor's four fingers, holding him tenderly.

*　　*　　*

Not all of Tenderville however wanted their thumbs stitched back on. Some people had learnt to live without their thumbs for such a long time, that they were happier without them. Some left their thumbs in the jar and put them in a display cabinet or up on the mantel piece. Some used their thumbs as ring holders, others to help prop up a slipping window pane, some fed their thumbs to the family dog, and it was discovered that thumbs also made brilliant door stoppers.

No matter what they chose to do with their thumbs, it was up to them, because it was their thumbs to do with as they pleased. Morden however could not have his thumbs stitched back on. Because the jar had broken, and the thumbs had dried in the air, because of this, they were no longer any good. But Morden, just like Archor, learnt to love his four fingered hands.

*　　*　　*

Mrs Chatelaine and Mr Hollingsworth were the first to ride the newly-opened tunnel-of-love, and the town all cheered and sprinkled them with pink blossom petals, and they started to kiss just as they disappeared into the darkness of the tunnel. This is something couples seem to do, when they have just got married! On the back of their boat was a sign that said *Just Married* painted by Garnet, Morden, Archor, Lilac and Lucidity.

Which made a perfect end to the day.

Late that afternoon, as the sun set and the sky filled with the glow of pink, Archor and Lilac hung the material drapes of cross stitched hopes in the orange trees. They both agreed that there were too many hopes to pin on one persons shoulders, and that the jacket would only become heavy to wear, and the fabric would get in the way of his magic tricks. So Lilac took the fabrics of multiple colours, with the carefully sewn words and hung them from the branches. The evening breeze flapped the material, and the words of hope fluttered in the air and filled the sky with colour and hope, and a feeling of lightness.

Lilac and Archor made a pinkie promise to always be friends, and you don't need thumbs to make a pinkie promise.

And everyone in the town of Tenderville, lived happily ever after.

𝕳𝖊𝖗𝖊 𝕰𝖓𝖉𝖊𝖙𝖍 𝕿𝖍𝖊 𝕬𝖗𝖈𝖍𝖔𝖗 𝕮𝖍𝖆𝖙𝖊𝖑𝖆𝖎𝖓𝖊 𝕳𝖎𝖘 𝕿𝖆𝖑𝖊

Epilogue.

Pickled Thumbs: not to be eaten with carrots, pasta or potatoes.
The myth behind the truth.

And so these are my four stories, and just like all fables, what went before is told a little differently. Klaus, Bella, and Fergus' stories sometimes get a little mixed up, and Archor's story is sometimes told through poetry, sometimes told to those that suck their thumb.

But like all myths, fables, legends and folklore, depending on customs and tradition, the story may alter, some changes are made, but the heart of the story is still there, and so is a small (mustard) seed of truth.

Here Endeth The Book